THE SOUL OF A MAN

AS TOLD TO

JIM EAGLE

BY

EL CAZADOR

A DOCUDRAMA IN PRINT

ISBN: 9798510935219 (Paperback)

Any references to historical events, real people, or real places are used fictitiously. Names, characters, and places are products of the author's imagination. (or are they?)

Front cover image by *Rusty Humphries*
Book design by *Gram Telen*
Sketches by *Igor Olszewski*
Edited by *Janille Dutton*
Additional editing *Rusty Humphries*

First printing 2021.

The Soul of a Man, LLC
6145 E Cave Creek Rd
Cave Creek, AZ 85331

⊕ www.TheSoulofaManBook.com

⊘ Thesoulofamanllc@gmail.com

Acknowledgments

I have spent a lifetime knowing I have something to say and to share. Hell, everyone has something to say. The question is, do people *want to hear it*? I have been writing for years—never sharing. I must have written over 100 poems, prose, and a couple of songs—even started two books that I never finished. Never having just "put it out there" to find out if people *want to hear it*.

THE SOUL OF A MAN began as self-therapy, a way to try to placate a troubled soul. Yet, as God's gift of *life in overtime* continues, it has somehow evolved into my first published work. This would never have occurred without the support, encouragement, and guidance of some very special people:

Jessyca Eagle-Quinn—my daughter, the love of my life, whose quiet encouragement and gentle nudges kept me moving forward.

Charlie Eagle—my son, the other love of my life. His artistic input and encouragement were priceless.

Barbara Eagle-Daley—my sister, whose support, memories, and creative social media talent have been a welcomed gift.

Rusty Humphries—my "Rockstar - publishing coach," whose knowledge, professionalism, and amazing ability to get it done propelled and guided us through the maze that is self-publishing.

Amanda Vandergriend—my friend, who was the first to read a not-yet-edited version of what was to become the book you are now holding. "I loved it! When is the next episode coming out?" was her response.

Janille Dutton—my copy editor. Her talent, encouragement, and patience with a first-time author were a welcomed push forward.

And of course, the LORD above . . .

I thank you, one and all.

Dedicated
to

The helpless child of God, never given a chance at life.

TABLE OF CONTENTS

FOREWORD

Who is the biggest buyer of books in the world? Amazon? Barnes and Noble? Costco?

Nope! It's toilet paper companies, so they can shred the books and let you wipe in comfort.

I mention that because a lot of books I am asked to read probably deserve to be Charmin.

In my many years on the radio, I've probably been given an average of five books a DAY to read. Let's do the math: 25 books a week x 4 weeks. That's 100 books a month x 12 months =

1,200 books a year. I started in radio in 1983 but really didn't start hosting my own talk radio show until 1995. So 1,200 x 25 years = 30,000 books!

I have been asked to read nearly 30,000 books in my talk radio career. DAMN!!!!! I've been busy!

That being said, of those 30,000 books, very few have stuck in my mind. A minuscule number of those have been *page-turners*. You know, the type of book you can't put down. You start reading and look up for a moment, only to realize you've been reading for a couple of hours and still don't want to stop.

That is the kind of book you have before you now—not the toilet paper kind, the *page-turner* kind.

As a radio personality, professional singer, #1 Amazon Best Selling Author, music producer, actor, VIP talent coach, etc., I have been blessed to have worked with many major entertainers in my life—people like Will Smith, Mark Wahlberg, Ryan Seacrest, Dick Clark, Casey Kasem, Rush Limbaugh, George Michael, Adam Sandler, Chris Farley, Suzanne Somers, Chuck Woolery, Amy Grant, Tony Orlando, Michael Damian, Governor Sarah Palin, Wilson-Phillips, Orson Scott Card, Vice President Mike Pence, and hundreds more, along with major corporations like Coca-Cola, Mercedes-Benz, Ford. And to quote the band Journey, "It goes on, and on, and on, and on."

I have had a backstage pass to the greatest entertainers and storytellers of our time. That being said, I can be a little jaded at times. I can't tell you the number of times I've heard, "I'm going to write a book!" I try to be encouraging, but most people just talk. Very few actually do.

When my friend Jim Eagle (now forever to be remembered as "This makes Jim Crow look like Jim Eagle." — President Joe Biden) told me he was writing a book, my first reaction was the same . . . "Uh, yah, good luck with that." And I forgot all about it. Well, Jim is a tenacious SOB and a darn good storyteller too. I had no idea! After months of cajoling, I got my copy and read it all on one flight to Kansas City. It was so good, I couldn't wait to land to give him my praises.

FOREWORD

The Soul of a Man, as told to Jim Eagle by "El Cazador," is like binging a great series on Netflix, hoping it never ends. When it does end, you actually miss the characters and can't wait for the next season. That's exactly how I felt when I finished this book: when will the next one come out? What happens next?

I've sat with Jim in the foothills of Cave Creek, Arizona, and seen the bottle of Miller Light and a shot of Baileys on a small round table to his right. Where fact and fiction meet . . . honestly, I don't know, but it's a heck of a ride from start to finish.

Rusty Humphries

Nationally Syndicated Radio Talk Show Host
Phoenix, Arizona, 2021

Author's Note

The author is a storyteller, and this is a work of fact and fiction intermingled. Intended to be thought-provoking and entertaining. Names, characters, businesses, events, and incidents are mainly the product of the author's imagination. Any similarity or reference to actual persons, places, or events is purely coincidental and/or purposed to intrigue and entertain the reader. Furthermore, any derogatory or offensive words, depictions, or statements are purposed to enhance and clarify the storyline and not intended to offend any race, religion, gender, or institution.

Fifty percent of all proceeds will be donated to several children's hospitals and care facilities across the United States, including, but not limited to, St. Catherine's Center For Children in Albany, New York; St. Jude Research Hospital in Phoenix, Arizona; St. Joseph's Children's Center in Phoenix, Arizona, and Shriners Hospitals for Children, Tampa, Florida.

—————❖—————

In the deepest recesses of the human mind, there is a mass of swirling turmoil where all thought, feeling, and emotion surrender their individuality to one unreachable concept.

The Soul of a Man

—————❖—————

THE ISLANDS

I had a beach house in Hawaii at the end of a small peninsula on the north shore of the island of Oahu.

It was a time of hippies and Marvin Gaye and long hair.

I lived with a dark-haired beauty named Katy.

There was a hammock strung between two palm trees and tide pools and miniature beaches in the backyard.

We loved and played in the sand and tide pools throughout the day and laughed and partied under the starlit nights.

It was a time of love and danger. It was a time of reckless youth.

I was in love with Katy. I was in love with danger.

I lived at the edge of the limit, where the future had no place.

2020
THE ORIGIN

In an old western mining town located deep in the foothills north of Phoenix, Arizona, an old man sits on the upper rear deck of his refurbished 1870s saloon, where he now makes his home, silently rocking in an old leather and cowhide oak rocking chair—a bottle of Miller Lite and a shot of Baileys on a small round table to his right.

A younger man sits in a similar old oak rocking chair—dead still—with a bottle of water on the same small round table to his left.

On the old man's side of the table sits a nickel-plated, .357 single-action, western-style revolver with wooden grips branded with an eagle on one side and a hawk on the other.

Bradley Cooper sings "Maybe It's Time" from a Bluetooth speaker—also on the small round table.

A dark and haunting painting of four mystical winged warriors on horseback hangs over the wood-burning fireplace behind the two rocking chairs and the weaponized table.

The old man stares pensively into the clouds. He is preparing to take a long journey. No need to pack, for the mind-traveler needs no luggage.

His voice reaffirms his age as he begins to speak slowly and thoughtfully. His fingers stroke his thick mustache, which extends to the bottom of his chin as if the motion is somehow opening the door behind which his life is locked, and his mind begins to bleed.

The younger man listens intently.

The North Shore

I was drowning, and I knew it. I was headed down for the third time—out of control, disoriented, and in a state of panic. I knew I was drowning and yet was not willing to bring myself under control. A strange mix of calm and fear filled my mind, as a cornucopia of dead and mutilated bodies and skeletons—some in ripped and torn military uniforms, along with small white and gold-trimmed coffins filled with zombie-like babies, some with two heads—drifted slowly through the warm Hawaiian waters surrounding me. All seemingly overlaid with a spirit-like vision of what appeared to be four mystical winged warriors on horseback—the smell of gunpowder and fresh-cut grass ever-present.

A strange peacefulness came over me as memories of horror, mayhem, and murder raced past as if I were reliving them all at once. Deep in the soul of death, I felt myself sinking to the depths of eternity with no lanterns to guide me—only the deep black of death calling.

Strangely, the four mystical winged warriors—armed with cross, sword, staff, and spear—seemed to be gently nudging me out of death's grip.

I was suddenly pushed up from below and brought to the surface, coughing and flailing and vomiting salt water.

"Goddamn it, John! What the fuck are you doing? Get your shit together!" was what I heard as I was pulled toward the shore and dragged up onto a moonlit Hawaiian beach on the north shore of the Island of Oahu.

As I spewed seawater and vomited uncontrollably, my two friends—and employees—who had just saved me from being tomorrow's headlines in the *Honolulu Gazette*, continued toward the beach house from which we had emerged forty-five minutes earlier, leaving me alone to self-recover and "get over it" in private. As they knew I would want to do.

It was the elaborate home of a local, well-heeled celebrity, whose drug-filled luau and a moonlit Hawaii night had given us the bright idea to go diving for lobster at 1:00 a.m., in a drug- and alcohol-induced state of euphoria.

Having regained my composure, I headed back to the house somewhat sober yet still in the border world I had entered thanks to the alcohol and chemicals I had ingested over the last several hours. As I entered the home and approached the thirty-foot-long bar filled with local party-goers, from a ten-year-old in a bathing suit smoking an acid-soaked joint at one end to an eighty-year-old man dressed in a butler's suit saturated with gin at the other, I could hear my "friends" Alex and Roy roaring with laughter and making fun of the "coast haole" (a white guy from California), whom they had just saved from his own stupidity. Me, of course.

As I approached the bar, now for the most part in control of myself and resuming my normal better-than-thou, quasi-badass attitude and persona, Katy smiled at me and raised her chin slightly.

"I'm good," I said as she pulled me close and let everyone know to whom she belonged. Her long black hair and hippy bangs surrounded a perfectly tanned, high-cheek-boned Southern California face. She was broadcasting a smile only possible when everyone else in the room fades from view, and all you see is the one you love—the one you love unconditionally. And fortunately for me, I was the lucky guy.

She was twenty-one years old and as beautiful inside as out. Perfect figure, long legs, five feet, eight inches tall with a young heart ready to love and care in the way only a young pure heart not yet scarred by tragedy and betrayal can do and free to feel and love with complete abandon. This was Katy, and I returned her love just as unconditionally, at least for the moment.

She handed me a beer and kissed my lips as only she could—a kiss that promised that there were bigger and better things to follow, whenever and wherever I wished to pursue them. I was in love with Katy. I was in love with the moment. And I was devoid of fear knowing full well the inevitability of sudden death and not caring when it came for me. There was no future, only now.

As Alex and Roy approached, I briefly wondered if I had been trying to die out there in the deep blue darkness. Dismissing the thought, I thanked them both yet jokingly told them not to do me any favors should that situation repeat itself.

It was at that moment that my world would begin to spin out of control.

A tall beefy Italian guy I did not know approached us. Looking straight at me, he said, "Dumb, fucking asshole. You should know better than to dive when you're fucked up."

"Who the fuck are you?" I replied.

"I'm the guy who is gonna bitch-slap you if—"

He didn't get any further. A swift right-hand to his nose and a well-placed kick in the balls abruptly turned him into a babbling crybaby with blood and snot spewing everywhere from his badly busted nose! As some other guests kindly guided him to the closest restroom, Katy gave me that "time to go" look. I smiled, took her hand, and over-politely said, "Good evening gentlemen," to Alex and Roy while heading for the door.

Once outside, I suddenly became uncontrollably obsessed with having sex with Katy. When we reached my '66 Mustang convertible in the driveway, I leaned her over the trunk of the car and lifted the silky summer dress she was wearing. Then I heard, "Hey, asshole, I'm gotta cut you and that haole (a white girl) whore-bitch until nobody can recognize either one of you!"

I turned to see the "goon" with the broken nose standing about thirty yards away with what appeared to be a machete in his hand. Instinct and nine years of living on the edge took over. Signaling Katy to move to the far side of the car, I quickly moved toward the driver's side of the Mustang, where I had a .357 Magnum stashed in the convertible's boot. Drawing the weapon, I turned to the asshole—whose nose had not yet stopped bleeding—just as he began to charge. *Don't kill him* was the message my brain sent to my right index finger, which was, at the moment, making love to the trigger of my .357. He was about fifteen yards away and charging at full speed like a madman when I calmly took aim at his left knee cap and blew it off. Large chunks of blood-splattered bone and skin exploded into the night air as the bullet hit its mark.

I figured I did him and myself both a favor—kept him out of the graveyard and me out of a messy situation that even "the KEEPER" may not be able to handle. He went down like the little bitch he was, screaming and crying that he couldn't believe that I had shot him.

Katy had the Mustang running and was behind the wheel when I leaped over the passenger door and slid into the seat. Before I could utter the words "let's get out of here," we were on the two-lane highway leading toward Haleiwa and Sunset Beach.

The past and the present were merging in a collage of images as we sped smoothly along the coast highway.

It will never be over for you, NewMex, were the words carved into the walls of the deepest caverns of my soul.

My current name is John Bridge, and I am not who I appear to be. To Alex, Roy, and Katy, and anyone else who knows me,

I am a tough-talking, easy-to-get-along-with but quick-to-anger, and even quicker-to-react owner of a rather large used car lot in Honolulu, Hawaii.

The year is 1971, I am twenty-seven years old, and I hold in my possession dark and unspeakable truths that can never be revealed. It is these secret truths that haunt me at the three o'clock hour of the morning—the darkest hour when the passions and horrors rise from the depths of our soul and remind us who we really are.

Perhaps, it is these secrets that cause me to feel the need to put myself in dangerous situations and make me wish I don't come out of them, for I have not yet learned to live with them or deal with them. My heart, I believe, is at war with my soul.

By the time we had arrived at our beach cottage just west of Sunset Beach, I was sobering up enough to reflect on what had just occurred. Not that I particularly gave a shit about the asshole I shot or the possible consequences, whether legal or retaliatory, I just didn't give a fuck.

Of course, I was not yet aware of who it was I had just crippled.

Katy and I lived in a one-bedroom cottage at the end of a small peninsula. Sunroom, breakfast nook and kitchen downstairs, bedroom upstairs. It was perfect for us—very private, with a lawn and palm trees in the backyard (two of which held a fishnet hammock) and beyond which there was a semi-rocky beach. At night when the tide came in, pools would form among the rocks as the sea hugged and caressed the shoreline and then flowed around and over the boulder-sized lava formations. In the morning, when the tide went out, miniature white sandy beaches appeared among the large rocks, providing several private, room-sized, white sand-carpeted areas in which to love and laugh and play. It was a place where your soul found time to speak to you, and the wounds in your heart found time to heal a little. It was, in fact, as close as I would ever get to any semblance of inner peace. It was our place, Katy's and mine. We were lovers there. We were children there. We were together there—alone in thought, but together.

We made love that night—not conventional lovemaking but rather a version of what the Japanese refer to in a much broader sense as "Shibumi," or the art of perfecting simplistic beauty. When applied sexually, it can be referred to as mental intercourse, wherein both participants must arrive at a sexual climax at the same time without talking to or touching each other or one's self—naked, kneeling on your heels about two feet apart, with minimal movement, direct eye contact, and mental sexual stimulation only. It is, without a doubt, one of the most gratifying forms of sex that a man and a woman can experience together.

It takes a profoundly personal and sexual bonding between the partners—extending through passion to the far side of obsession—plus practice, concentration, imagination, and level-III climax control (sometimes hovering at the edge of climax while waiting for your partner to reach their point of hovering). As it is a revised version of "Kikashi sex," which itself is a revision within level-IV Japanese lovemaking, it is rarely achieved—most generally resulting in both parties giving tacit consent to revert to conventional sex games. To actually achieve "sexual Shibumi" or Kikashi sex, both parties must reach an organism at the exact same moment. Katy and I had had only one successful Kikashi after thirty-five minutes of intense mind-over-body control. It was such an unbelievable experience that we seemed to chase after it ever since by starting each romantic encounter in this manner. On this particular night, perhaps due to the excessive amounts of alcohol, drugs ingested, and turn of events, we lasted only about five minutes before we reverted to some basic, raw fucking. Which, of course, achieved the same results, less the mental satisfaction that Kikashi sex brings but quite satisfying, nonetheless.

Goddamn! She was a great piece of ass!

With the coming of the dawn, the miniature beaches reappeared in the backyard along with the annoying reality of a ringing phone, and a ringing phone at 7 a.m. on a Sunday was not a good thing.

It was Alex.

Alex Kono was a born-and-bred Hawaiian who worked as one of my managers at THE CAR LOT. I had met Alex at a bar in Waikiki the first night I arrived on the island. He was young, energetic, good looking, and very street savvy. It was a game of pool that got us talking, and as it turned out, he knew everyone on the island, most of whom were his cousins—or so he kept saying. It was his connections that had enabled me to open my car lot so quickly. We had it up and running and turning a profit within three months of my arrival. And now, it was those same "cousin" connections that were about to save my ass.

"The asshole with the broken nose and missing kneecap is known to my cousin Benny, who works Honolulu Vice Squad. Apparently, he is a badass from the mainland who has friends in high political places within the Vietnamese government. He's been on the island for about two days and has been asking a lot of questions about a certain haole who owns 'THE CAR LOT' in Honolulu. That would be you, JB."

"He told my cousin he has friends who are interested in your time as an Army Ranger in Vietnam. Says you were involved with some heavy shit in and around Cambodia during the Vietnam War. Is that true? You never mentioned it."

"I was never in the army, let alone a Ranger in Vietnam. So, what else did he say?"

"Says this guy's superiors are trying to fill in some gaps in your past, and the guy doesn't seem to know why. Guess he's just a mutt, a high-dollar gopher if you will. My cousin says he heard about what happened last night, but nobody's reported it, so no one is looking for you. He does say that this badass you seem to have turned into a gimp is not the type to let it go. Says maybe you might—*should* have killed him."

"Says he'll keep me posted when the guy checks in again. In the meantime, he says you need to watch your back. This guy is high-dollar dangerous and heavily connected. He doesn't see him letting it go any time soon. Also wants me to let you know that if all this bullshit interrupts his getting stoned and cruising through life that he will not be happy."

"Alright, Alex, thank you, and thank your 'cousin.' Are you at the lot?"

"No, it's Sunday. We're closed."

"Oh, well, I thought perhaps you were showing a little initiative and opening up on Sunday."

"With all due respect, boss, fuck you."

"Hahaha! Have a great day off, Alex, and thanks again for being my archangel and saving my life on a regular basis. Would you knock it off? I'm trying to die!"

As I hung up the phone, the doorbell rang. It was Roy.

Roy was another guy whom I had met shortly after arriving on the Islands. He was five feet eight with about forty years' worth of rock-hard neck muscle and an attitude to match. We had met in a bar—yes, I spend a lot of time in bars. He'd been sitting a couple of stools down from me in this dive gin joint out by the airport when a six-foot-five, three hundred pound Samoan seated on the other side of me decided—in his drunken stupor— that I was everything he hated about haoles. He proceeded to indulge himself in ridiculing all white guys, which he somehow had assumed "I" represented. I smiled and nodded and tried to placate and ignore him at the same time, as he looked just a little large for me to handle without causing a whole lot of commotion. I was there just to have a quiet beer and work through my advertising budget for the upcoming month. Now, just as I was deciding that this fucking Samoan needed a lesson in manners, I see Roy stand up and leave. *Guess my fellow haole saw trouble coming and didn't want any part of it.*

"Hey, fucking haole!" the monster to my right said to me, "I'm gonna fuck you up."

Just then, the door opened, and Roy let out with a whistle that is typically used to call a dog. The gorilla and I both turned and look at him, wondering which one of us he was calling to.

"You! The big fucking dumb Samoan, get the fuck out here!"

I was thinking, *what the fuck is this*?

The Samoan said, "Guess that other dumb fucking haole wants his ass kicked first," and headed for the door at the end of the bar about twenty feet from where I was sitting. He opened the door, and the next thing I knew, the asshole Samoan was flailing backward with his arms waving in the air like a pigeon attempting to perform a reverse landing. He tried, unsuccessfully, to stay on his feet as he went past me and finally crashed into the jukebox and slid clumsily to the floor.

Roy said, "You might want to get out of here before that stupid fuck wakes up unless you feel like wrestling with an angry gorilla." Once outside, Roy said, "If you want to have a quiet beer, there's an upscale restaurant just down the street with a great lounge called The South Seas. If you want to slide down there, I'll buy you a beer."

"I'll meet you there, but I owe you the beer. Great right cross you got there," I said, referring to the punch he landed, which had sent the Samoan twenty feet backward.

"That was a left jab, son," he responded with a smirk on his face. "The right drops them where they stand."

It was the beginning of a great friendship, although one that Roy, unfortunately, would not survive.

"Hey, Roy, come on in."

"I don't want to disturb your Sunday, boss. Just checking on you. Did Alex fill you in on the guy you shot?"

"Yeah, he said he's some goon from the mainland."

"Yeah, a badass heavily connected goon who has been asking a lot of questions about you, from what I hear."

"Yeah, well, between his knee and his nose, I suspect he'll be off the streets for a few days. Want a beer?"

"Sure. I'm sure it's happy hour somewhere."

Just then, Katy came down the stairs rocking a tank top and a pair of short shorts that could not possibly be unhappy with their current assignment. I made a mental note to say a prayer that I might be reincarnated as a pair of short shorts owned by Katy! She came directly over to me, displaying body language and a smile that only a woman who had most recently been fully sexually satisfied could display, and said, "Hi babe. You guys want some breakfast?" as she kissed me on the lips, with her body fully against mine and then headed to the kitchen. *Goddamn*, I thought. If Roy weren't here, I'd take her right back upstairs, at the same time wondering if she was actually as beautiful and sexy as I thought she was or if I was just so in *love* with her that I only saw what I wanted to see. No matter. It worked for us both at the moment, and for me at least, the moment is all there is. I live in the present. For the future—including the next minute—was nonexistent for me. The future is right now.

Roy and I each grabbed a cold bottle of Miller Lite and wandered out into the backyard to enjoy the ocean as Katy began cooking up what was starting to smell like a great breakfast feast. Unbelievable, she cooks too!

"Tell me if it's none of my business," Roy said, "but what the fuck is going on here? Last night, you walk away from what was nothing short of a thwarted suicide attempt only to totally fuck up a guy who turns out to be a heavyweight government badass investigating you. And you, according to the Honolulu PD, are some ex-Army Ranger badass with a hole in his past. Am I fucking dreaming or what?"

You must "never" let anyone know anything about you or your past. Always stay in the present. You are who you appear to be, period!

"To tell you the truth, Roy, I have no fucking idea what the fuck they're all talking about. I have never even been in the army, let alone the Army Rangers. I was first married when I was eighteen years old and received a 3-A draft classification, which kept me out of the military altogether. I've never been to Cambodia or even Vietnam, for that matter. Looks like a case of mistaken identity to me, nearest I can figure."

"Not that I don't believe you, boss, but you sure look like someone who's been trained in how to fight and use a weapon. The way you dispatched the guy last night was slick. One quick stiff arm to the nose and it was broken. One perfectly placed shot to the knee cap, and it was gone. Damned impressive, I'd say."

"Well, thanks for the compliment, I think. But I was never in the army. As for training, I grew up in New York. I was on the streets at eight years old. You learn to defend yourself real quick in that environment—fists, sticks, rocks, knives, and guns. You learn it all, or you don't survive—comes in handy sometimes."

"I guess it does, boss. I guess it does. I'm glad you're on my team, or I should say, I'm glad I'm on your team?"

"So, what's next? What are we gonna do about this 'mistaken identity' thing?"

If they ever come for you, stay in character, and I'll reach out. Remember, stay in character at all costs.

"Well, I figure we'll be a little extra cautious, keep selling a lot of cars, and let the Honolulu PD sort it out."

The smell of bacon 'n' eggs and toast and coffee had increasingly grown stronger as we talked—to the point that it could no longer be ignored.

"Let's eat," I said, ending a potentially dangerous conversation.

Six Days Later, Saturday, 7:30 a.m.

The Car Lot was fast becoming the number one used car operation on the island of Oahu, with an inventory of over three hundred cars and an advertising budget of $100,000 per month. I was turning three hundred units a month at an average gross profit of $3,000 per unit for a total gross profit of $900,000 per month. This had been accomplished in just a little over twelve months on the island. I was not happy about the prospect of having to shut it down and disappear into the mist when I was netting over $100,000 per month!

"Mornin' boys and girls! We ready to crank it up today? It's Saturday, ladies and gentlemen, and Saturday is game day. We need a minimum of fifty units today. That's two units each, so if you're hungover or your ass is draggin', do whatever it is you need to do—coke, bennies, weed, whatever is gonna get you crankin'! By 9:00 a.m., this place will be crawling with buyers, and we don't want to miss any of them, so get your shit together and your attitudes straight! Make it happen. We hit fifty units, and there is a $100 cash spiff for every unit sold. That's over and above commissions and bonuses and payable in cash on your way out the door tonight. Leave before we hit fifty, and you get nothing!

"So let's make it happen, ladies and gentlemen. And remember, buyers are liars, so *no* means *yes*. And with our $100,000 advertising budget and average monthly sales of 300 units, that means that every swingin' dick that walks on the lot costs me $333 to get him here for you. So if any of you let a customer go without first turning them to another sales person, you owe me $333—payroll deductible, or just go ahead and leave with them.

"Now, let's go. I want every car unlocked and started before the customers get here. So let's make it happen, ladies and gentlemen. We need a day!"

Call me sick, but I love the goddamn car business!

As Alex hustled everybody out the door and Roy passed out cross-top bennies (speed) to anyone who wanted them, I was headed back to my office when I heard, "Mr. Bridge, telephone call, line two, please. Mr. Bridge, line two, please."

"John Bridge, here. How can I help you?"

"Be at the Chart House at Ali Wai Yacht Harbor at midnight." *Click.*

It was the KEEPER, and I knew he was correct: it was time to go. Someone had the scent. Someone was too close. It was time for John Bridge to disappear and someone else to emerge somewhere else—different name, different game, same MO. Make money, enjoy life, and stay deep.

This is not easy, I thought, as I went to the safe in the floor of the storage shed in the back of the lot. But it pays well!

Never take more than $100,000 in cash for pocket change. I'll retrieve the rest and bring it to you.

In this case, the *rest* was close to $2.4 million—between what I had brought from Riverside, California, and the profits made in Hawaii.

I had no problem with following the rules, as I knew the KEEPER would see that the balance arrived wherever I landed.

The fact that the meeting was set at midnight, the harbor was code for "your cover had been blown; you're leaving tonight."

No goodbyes, no I love yous, no thank-yous, no luggage. I must carry on through the day as I usually would, and in the morning, a mutilated body would be found and identified as John Bridge, owner of THE CAR LOT in Honolulu. Alex and Roy would mourn. Katy would cry. And me, I would become someone else, somewhere else, and this would continue until I managed to find an identity that would not be compromised.

Such is the reality of my existence—never *really* loving, never *really* caring, never growing any permanent roots.

I arrived at the Chart House at 11:55 p.m., having left the lot at 11:10 p.m. after a sixty-two-car day—$186,000 I would never see. As I approached the bar, a very pretty young woman with an uncanny resemblance to Katy casually bumped into me and spilled her martini on my shirt.

Apologizing profusely, she insisted on buying me a drink. I agreed, but only if she joined me. She nodded her approval as we sat down at the bar.

"Do you know who I am?" she whispered.

"I assume you are connected to the KEEPER, yes?"

"Exactly. We'll have a couple or more drinks, enjoy a bit of laughter together, which will lead to romance and then leave together, and I will become the mysterious women you left the bar with. At dawn, a body will turn up on the beach and be identified as John Bridge, and your true identity will never be discovered."

"Yes, ma'am! I know the drill. Cheers."

THE CROSSING

I awoke around 11:30 a.m. the next day. Leilani was her name, the girl from the Chart House. She was a classy lady and possessed a level of intellect and savvy that I found quite attractive. Apparently, she was to be my traveling companion for the next few days as we sailed across the Pacific.

After leaving the Chart House, we had boarded a 57-foot ketch aptly named *Dauntless*.

It was my way to get high, drunk, and laid whenever I needed to escape the reality of the life I was destined to lead. Judging from my lack of memory concerning events after I boarded the *Dauntless*, the pounding headache I was experiencing, and the smiling beauty lying next to me, I must have accomplished my mission: we were somewhere in the middle of the Pacific.

I could feel it coming on, that sad and depressing feeling of loneliness. It was all gone again. I knew better than to allow this feeling to get a grip on me, so I bounced out of bed and grabbed a Miller Lite out of the fridge and headed for the shower.

Three beers, a joint, and a nice breakfast of burnt bacon and three fried eggs over medium found me sitting on the rear deck, contemplating the vastness and the loneliness at the heart of the sea. I am haunted by the sea. I have always gravitated to her in awe and fascination, feeling content and at peace only when I am in her arms.

My thoughts were suddenly interrupted.

"The KEEPER," Leilani said, as she handed me the phone.

"I need a name and a destination within the next twenty-four hours." *Click!*

Not one to mince words, I thought with a slight smile on my face. But of course, he was correct: I needed to decide on a new identity and a destination so he could prepare all the documents and back up stories I would need to create a walk-on for my new life.

THE BAY

It had been another grueling yet rewarding day at the office. Yet as I walked along the shore of the bay, I could feel the stress almost running from my body. A Miller Lite in my left hand, a joint in my right hand, and a Barnes & Noble bag with two more beers slung over my shoulder might just have something to do with this feeling of contentment and freedom. Or was it just the sea? When I am in her presence, I have an overwhelming feeling of relief and freedom. I love the sea. She is my secret mistress. When away from her, I am lost and anxious as I also suffer from an extreme form of claustrophobia and must be on the edge of the continent to feel truly free.

The sand under my feet, the refreshing July breeze off the ocean, the salty smell of the sea. . . . I was where I needed to be, "in the moment," living only for this moment in time. This feeling of freedom and bliss is what I live for; all the rest is just time passing.

It was 1:00 a.m. Another seventeen-hour day spent building a new business from the ground up—this time an auto leasing brokerage in San Diego, California. Realizing I was roughly about a half-mile away from my condo, I reversed direction and headed back down the beach regretting that I needed to let go of my current state of contentment and get some sleep. Six o'clock in the morning came around early.

I had arrived back at my condo around 1:30 a.m., not getting to sleep till about 2:00 a.m. Now, sitting in my office at 7:15 a.m., I was struggling through my second cup of coffee, trying to get ready for my daily 7:30 a.m. sales meeting. I needed to get twenty-one salespeople pumped up and ready for another day of prospecting for and closing leases on new vehicles. Interesting and a little tricky, as we did not inventory any vehicles.

First, we found the client—mostly upscale, well-to-do folks who liked to be catered to. We secured an order for a specific vehicle, then purchased the vehicle from a new car fleet dealer and delivered it to the client for a tidy profit. *It was all about service* and rubbing shoulders with the well-heeled upper crust.

I had decided on San Diego during the crossing from Hawaii. It is on the ocean, on the border, and has the best weather in the USA. Why not?!

When we docked at Glorietta Bay on Coronado Island just south of downtown San Diego, Leilani stayed with the boat, and I was handed a leather bag with $2.4 million in cash and a new identity. I am now Tim Hawk. Everything else was up to me—the what, the when, and the how.

I checked into the Hotel del Coronado and proceeded to the bar. It was a sunny Sunday morning in March, and the weather was superb.

I stayed a couple of weeks, using the telephone and my determination to remake my life and to set up a new business. I positioned my offices in Mission Valley, a burgeoning hub of commerce slightly northeast of downtown San Diego.

I purchased a penthouse condo on Sail Bay in Pacific Beach and preceded to establish my new identity as a young—aggressive, if not a bit crass—businessman with a limited past.

Business was immediately profitable. An unknown $2.5 million did wonders to help make me look like an excellent businessman with a knack for success; although, within a very short time, I was turning a pre-tax profit of over $30,000 per month. It was not yet the $100,000 plus I was netting in Hawaii but respectable, nonetheless.

Over the next year, I continued to grow my company, Coastal Auto Leasing Company Inc., and established myself in the San Diego community. I had altered my appearance to the point of unrecognizable as the now-deceased "John Bridge." My new identity had proven secure at every turn, from social security number to driver's license to credit to family background, etc. The KEEPER knows his job and is very good at it. I was beginning to feel secure again but cautious, ever-cautious, always watching, always looking. Paranoia was my bodyguard.

Still is!

Just because I'm paranoid doesn't mean they're not coming for me.

Thoughts of Hawaii and Katy and Alex and Roy took turns popping from my memory caverns to the front of my mind. I had positioned them in a special place there—not locked but secure.

I had learned that following my untimely demise, Alex and Roy had attempted to exact revenge on the goon from the mainland—apparently assuming he had been responsible for my death—resulting in a bloody battle at THE CAR LOT. The goon was cut in half by two vehicles sandwiching him to death. It wasn't hard to figure who was driving them. Roy lost his life in the exchange, and Alex has vanished.

Thank you, Roy, for your loyalty. Rest in peace.

Alex, wherever you are, I hope we meet again at the after-party. I love you, dude. Stay safe!

As for Katy, she most likely moved back to the mainland, probably somewhere in California. I still feel a love for her, but my drive to survive in the world I have chosen forbids any future contact and overrides all else.

I do continue to wonder, however, just how well she is dealing with my death, given the news story on how I was last seen in the early morning hours leaving the Chart House with a beautiful unidentified woman and then found mutilated on the beach.

I can only imagine the cornucopia of feelings she has been forced to deal with. Bittersweet at best. "Life's a bitch, and then you die."

1973

It's Sunday morning. I'm sitting on my patio by the sea, where I belong, drinking my fourth Miller Lite of the day and smokin' a doobie—the absolute best remedy for a hangover you'll ever find. I've gone from feeling like I'm inches from death to a pleasant buzz in less than an hour. It's a gorgeous day on the bay, a sunny 86°F with a wisp of a salty breeze coming in off the ocean. The bay is calm as the two-inch-high ripples lay themselves gently on the shore.

Just as I'm slightly dozing and enjoying a warm feeling of peacefulness, *she* appears!

Out of my semi-open right eye, I see what, at first, I believe to be an illusion brought on by my newly acquired buzz resulting from the aforementioned ingredients, which have combined with the place, the day, and the mood.

She is so hot! And she lives next door!

As it turns out, her name is Roxzanne Stillwell, and she and her husband, Ron, own a chain of sixty TV and appliance stores. She has an air of sophistication coupled with a girl-next-door smile, along with jet-black hair and a very sexy and deeply tanned body, which is quite visible clad only in a skimpy, black bikini.

My sudden arousal slightly calms as her husband appears. His appearance and demeanor are the male match to hers. They look like they belong together, which tends to chill my interest. I am not one to come between a happy couple. I'm both appreciative and envious of such relationships. Not wanting to interfere with their apparent happiness, I close my eyes, but I still see her.

"Hey, babe, you doin' okay?"

It's Diana, a twenty-one-year-old stripper I brought home with me a couple of weeks ago from a high-dollar gentlemen's club in the suburbs of San Diego. A great piece of ass but way too crass and uneducated to keep around for too long. She definitely does not possess the attributes required to accompany me on the journey I am embarking on, one which would lead me to the upper edge of San Diego society. I like her, but I know I will have to lose her soon. Too bad—a great fuck, and I like her, but she had to go.

Sometimes I wonder what the hell is wrong with me. But knowing the list is too long, I retreated from the thought.

As I soak in the day, the place, the women, and the booze, I decide I need a boat. I have a dock that comes with the condo, so I'm surprised I didn't realize this sooner.

The LadyHawk

Monday afternoon finds me test sailing a twenty-seven-foot Pacific Dolphin sloop off the coast of Oceanside, California.

She's a beauty—large enough for extended trips to Catalina Island or Ensenada, Mexico, yet compact and maneuverable enough to navigate the waters of San Diego and Mission Bays.

I mount a spread-winged brass hawk to her transom and name her *LadyHawk*—suitable to her beige hull and extensive teak trim and makes her an instant partner in life.

I'm becoming quite comfortable in my new life. Now, if I do my job keeping my true identity buried and the KEEPER has done his by backing up my new identity with a traceable family and past, maybe, just maybe, I can build something that will last.

Although visions of death and mayhem continue to haunt my thoughts, I'm starting to believe in a future. Dangerous for me!

Perhaps I am learning not to wait for the storm to pass but rather to enjoy dancing in the rain.

We shall see. . . .

1962

It's a boy, but there's a problem!

He will not live a year. I will weep uncontrollably for hours over his grave and leave the cemetery a different person—no longer an innocent eighteen-year-old youth comfortable with a predictable future but rather a man with a vengeance and a hatred for all that is sacred and warm and comforting. I will become a man bent on self-destruction, a man who will refuse to feel or care or love, a man seeking to destroy anything or anyone connected to the life he has been denied. I will embark upon an irreversible journey.

A stranger in the cemetery observes as four mystical winged warriors on horseback surround the boy.

THE BREAKERS

I'm sailing the *LadyHawk* off the coast of La Jolla. It's a perfect July day—a 10-knot breeze out of the southwest and a cloudless 87°F. And I'm not alone. Marcy and Samantha (Sam) are their names—both young, both topless, both third-year college students at San Diego State University, and both a pleasure to look at.

We are all a little high on cocaine, weed, and beer—Lite beer by Miller, of course.

At the moment, Marcy is at the helm, and Sam is happily occupied, making sure that I do not want for sexual satisfaction.

Just when I'm basking in the fact that "it just doesn't get any better than this," I hear a bullhorn announcing, "Ahoy there, *LadyHawk!*"

I pull on my swim trunks, and coming topside, I'm staring at two harbor patrol cops in their patrol boat not twenty yards away.

"What's the problem, officer?" I manage to say in as sober a voice as I can muster. Marcy reaches for her bikini top—almost in slow motion as she observes the two well-tanned, good-looking officers in the patrol boat, who are both presenting her with their best smiles.

"You might want to look quickly to your starboard side, sir."

As I turn, I am staring at a five-foot swell about to crest just six feet from my sloop, threatening to swamp her. "Shit" seems to be the only word I have time for as I dive for the helm, pushing Marcy aside and hitting the starter button for the motor at the same time. The *LadyHawk* instantly responds as I spin her wheel hard to port, and her prop bites deep into the sea, now raising on the outside edge of the cresting five-foot breaker. She grips the top of the churning wave, not ten seconds from cresting. A 180-degree swing of the wheel to the starboard finds us gliding down the backside of the wave at a 45-degree angle, swooping through the trough, and climbing the next incoming swell at the same 45-degree angle. We smoothly crest that threat and descend on into the next few less-precarious swells until we once again find ourselves outside of the breakers in calm seas, and the *LadyHawk* is smiling.

The harbor patrol pulls within about twenty-five yards, and once again, using their bullhorn, announces, "Nicely done, captain. I think maybe *you* need to man the helm, sir. Good day, ladies. It's been a pleasure assisting you today."

Sam had come topside, not bothering with her bikini top as both girls wave happily at the officers. I'm not quite sure if they are happy that they left without boarding us and finding several illegal substances or if they were trying to impress them with their beauty and availability. Either way, I just smiled as I shut down the motor, trimmed the mainsail, and set a course northeast toward Black's Beach—a nude beach on the eastern edge of La Jolla.

Of all the lease companies in all the towns in all the world, she walks into mine?

ROXZANNE

"Morning, boss. You got time to interview a friend of a friend of mine who's been going through some rough times and needs a gig?"

It's Jim Waters, my sales manager, and he knows I'm a sucker for a good sob story.

"What's his story?"

"Her story," he corrects.

"Her story?"

"Yeah, husband was Ron Stillwell. You know, the dude who owned all those TV and appliance stores until it went upside down a few months ago. Well, apparently, that business was not particularly on the up-and-up. So when it went under, he fled to Mexico, leaving her holding the bag. She's been fighting through all the legal bullshit; she's a tough broad. Now, she's running short of cash and thinks she can lease cars for us and make "us" and her a bunch of money, at least that's what she says."

"Wait a minute, Jimmy, what's her name, Roxzanne?"

"Yeah, you know her?"

"I've seen her around. Show her in."

She is beautiful in an exotic and sexual sort of way—salty black hair, pouty lips, a perfect figure, and eyes that strip you naked and then appraise you slowly, top to bottom and back up again!

I am suddenly in love again, and now she is available!

Two Months Later

I'm looking through the scope mounted on the top of a 30.06 Winchester at Roxzanne and two dudes settling a two-kilo cocaine deal in the living room of a beach house on one of several bays in the Mission and Pacific Beach area of San Diego. I'm lying spread-eagle on the deck of the *LadyHawk* in the middle of the bay, a large beach towel covering both my head and the muzzled barrel of the 30.06. Turns out, the lovely Roxzanne had become a cocaine dealer after the demise of her husband's TV empire to sustain herself in time of monetary distress, and her job as one of my leasing agents was secured as a cover.

Today finds me deeply involved in guaranteeing her safe return to the boat. My love of danger, easy money, and "lines on the mirror" twenty-four hours a day made it easy for me to become concerned with her safety, not to mention her beauty, her perverse sexual preferences, and our shared fondness for living on the edge.

My view through the upstairs window into the living room is crystal clear through the Smith and Wesson high-powered

Super x5 scope I had custom mounted on my Winchester. Always looking for action, I'm not quite sure if I'm hoping things go smoothly or not, but it's not my choice. And there it is! A .45 Automatic appears in the hand of one of the two dudes. Left without another option, I squeeze the trigger as flashbacks and vivid memories of a similar scene years before come streaming through my mind—the smell of the grass, the taste of brass, and "the boss is dead?"

Pop!

The shot is true. A direct hit to the shoulder supporting the pistol, and it goes flying as the other dude hits the deck. Roxzanne scoops up the coke and the money and exits the scene.

As previously planned, in the event of shots fired, Roxzanne exits quickly on the street side of the beach house and calmly proceeds eastward down the sidewalk as I set sail in the same direction.

Two blocks and seven minutes later, I've anchored the *LadyHawk,* and I'm rowing the dingy toward the shoreline as Roxzanne approaches. She is as cool as they get, smiling and waving as if it were a prearranged date.

We row out and board the *LadyHawk* and slowly sail north, assuming the appearance of a couple enjoying an afternoon sail on the bay.

She has the coke, the $40,000 in cash, and a very sexy smile on her face.

She may just be a cross between the daughter of the devil and an angel in white, but goddamn, you gotta like this chic!

Cambodia, August 1963

The VC are everywhere—fifty, maybe sixty of them. They have the Seventh Army's Recon Patrol surrounded.

His job: kill them all before they kill the seven members of the patrol.

He is nineteen years old, and he is a "deep black" Special Ops Army Ranger with a degree in killing. He's the Seventh Infantry Division's archangel assigned to tail them undetected and protect them from an unobserved, elevated position in the event that a deadly situation—similar to the one unfolding—should arise.

Pop, pop, pop! Three Cong dead!

He takes a breath, refusing to think!

Pop, pop, pop, pop!

Over and over again, until forty-eight are dead. He now relaxes as he watches the patrol gain control of the battle. Within the next five minutes, it's over. Fifty-two dead, six captured—then executed—all in a day's work. The patrol goes home, not quite sure exactly what happened, perhaps thinking, *Maybe the rumors are true—an angel watches over them!*

The shooter fades back into the jungle, alone with his demons.

Visions of small coffins haunt him through the deep-green and purple jungle night.

He is in a world of his own choosing, overflowing with guilt, shame, longing, bitterness, and vengeance—at war with the world and the god who rules it.

He is a soul shaper reshaping his soul as well as the souls of those he encounters.

Four mystical winged warriors surround him in the mist.

October 1963, Stateside

"Forgive me, sir, but the mission you have just described seems to contradict my understanding of just who I am working for."

"I am your immediate superior," replies the KEEPER. "You receive the orders you have sworn to follow from me, and you do not ever question those orders! Is that clear, NewMex?"

"Yes, sir! Perfectly clear, sir!"

It was that terse conversation that would haunt me for the rest of my life while securing my commitment to a simple and straightforward idiom that had been given to me by the KEEPER early in our relationship: "Loose lips sink ships." This kill was never, ever to be mentioned again! Although, worldwide speculation over who pulled the trigger would persist indefinitely—hopefully forever.

NEWPORT BEACH

1975

"Well, Mr. Tim Hawk, if you're here to convince me not to kill you, let's get started!"

I had walked into the lion's den, and the lion was vicious and deadly. My most prevalent thought: *Fuck him!* Any piece of shit, would-be hitman who would allow his prey into his home without a thorough search was a pussy, and here I was sitting in his study with a five-shot Bond Arms derringer in my boot. *Fuck him.* He'll be lucky if I don't decide to end his life before he decides whether or not to accept the contract that he has been offered to end mine.

His name is Billy Sanchez. He makes his home in Newport Beach, and he is a killer. But he is also a fiercely loyal friend to those he has allowed into his inner circle. And to my good fortune, Roxzanne is one of those who enjoys that loyalty.

It's been two years since she walked into my offices in Mission Valley, and we are still laughing, loving, and enjoying each other.

And I am still Tim Hawk!

The KEEPER keeps.

Perhaps like me, he is learning along the way, or perhaps he had nothing left to learn. Either way, here I am, now, all of a sudden, staring down the three-inch barrel of a nickel-plated .357 revolver built for short-range work.

"Please, Mr. Hawk, remove the derringer from your left boot and set it here on my desk."

Oh well, so much for the pussy theory. It becomes a bit clearer why he holds Roxzanne among his most trusted confidants.

"I'd much rather just keep it where it is, comfortably resting in its nest, if you don't mind."

"Put the fucking gun on my desk, Mr. Hawk!"

"Fuck you, Mr. Sanchez. It stays where it is. If you're not comfortable enough with the advantage you already have over me, then pull the fucking trigger and make yourself feel better."

It is one of those moments. The air is thick with indecision radiating from both men. Balls are being weighed against intellect, and both of us are enjoying the high-intensity match.

Who the fuck does this guy think he is? I'm the fucking badass in the room!

"Okay, Mr. Hawk, but the slightest movement in the direction of that derringer, and I'll blow your fucking head off and collect my payment from Mr. Feldman, who would be more than happy to pay me the $250,000 price tag he has put on your head."

I nod.

"Roxzanne suggested I meet you before I decided on the contract I was offered. I have a great deal of respect for Roxzanne and her judgment in such matters. So here we are, Mr. Hawk. Now tell me why I shouldn't collect the $250,000?"

"You should do what the fuck ever you want to do, 'Mr. Sanchez.' She told me she wanted me to meet you and that if we met, she knew you would pass on the contract, and 'I' would not have to kill 'you!' You see, she's not trying to protect me; she's trying to protect you! She also figured that our meeting might eventually prove beneficial to both of us.

"So here we are. Now either pull that fucking trigger or buy me a beer. Your choice. Personally, I'm thirsty, and I'm bored. So, either choice works for me."

He lowers his weapon.

"You in love with Roxzanne?"

"Love is for fools!"

"Roxzanne was correct; you are indeed an interesting man. It would be a shame to kill you. The cabinet to your left is a refrigerator. There's cold Miller Lite in there if you would be kind enough to grab two while you're there. I'm a bit thirsty myself. So, why does Feldman want you dead?"

"He's a poor loser."

"He said you stole his San Diego auto leasing business and merged it with yours."

"Payback's a bitch. He shorted me $36,000 on a business deal. I got even."

"I believe his business was worth maybe ten times that amount, and that's on a yearly basis, no?"

"As I said, payback's a bitch."

"Cheers!"

We chatted about nothing for about five Miller Lites, shook hands, and parted ways.

There was no further discussion about whether or not he would accept the contract, but we both knew that it would be best for all if he did not.

The next day, Roxzanne and I are enjoying the drive back down to San Diego. I had lowered the top on the brand new black Corvette convertible I had purchased a couple of weeks ago—a completely redesigned model that rivaled anything on the road in both speed and style. We are cruising at a refreshing 90 mph on the Pacific Coast Highway through Camp Pendleton just north of Oceanside, soaking up the sun and basking in the sights and sounds and smells of the sea immediately to our right. Ever vigilante, I had been observing a vehicle, now recognizable as a late-model Chevy sedan, slowly gaining on us in the center lane, which is what had alerted me, as it would have to be doing 100 mph plus to accomplish that task. Either it was someone in a hopped up Chevy who wanted to pit a custom-built street demon against the abilities of an assembly line speedster, or it was a problem.

As it approached, I increased our speed to 105 mph to test its intentions. It immediately came alongside the Vette and began edging me toward the concrete center divider. I was maybe six inches from slamming into the divider when I pulled my .380 from its holster under the steering column. I told Roxzanne to lean back and fired three rounds at his (or her) head, which was covered in a ski mask and a baseball cap. I floored the Vette. When I looked at the speedometer, it read 140 mph. A quick look in the passenger side mirror displayed a view of the would-be assassin veering off the highway and damned near ending up in the ocean.

As we reached the end of Camp Pendleton and approached the beach town of Oceanside, I selected an alternate inland route to complete our journey.

As I sat on my bayside patio later that night, reflecting on the weekend's events, I debated who the attempted assassin might have been. Was it from the past, from Sanchez, from Feldman, from Roxzanne's drug deal? Sanchez was my guess. After all, $250,000 is a lot of money. Fuck friendships!

What a shame. I rather liked him.

If it had any connection to the past, my phone would ring, and I would soon be on the move again. If no call, I would need to follow up. Was Sanchez the driver of the car? Had one or more of my shots fired killed him? If not, I would have to finish him off before he came at me again.

Just then, I felt the sensual hands of Roxzanne on my shoulders.

"You good, babe?" she said.

"Never better. You?"

"Just another day in paradise," she said as she sat down next to me and handed me a small round mirror with several lines of cocaine on it.

"Sanchez?!" she said.

I nodded.

She sighed.

The next day's headlines in the *San Diego Tribune* read:

"Newport Beach Man Shot to Death at Camp Pendleton"

The subsequent story identified him as William Sanchez, an entrepreneur from Newport Beach.

Good. But that still left Feldman to be dealt with.

The next day finds me sitting on a mountain top back in Newport Beach surveying Feldman's multimillion-dollar cliffside home. It was perfect. His pool was surrounded by an elaborate redwood deck that extended over the edge of the cliff. If someone were to fall from it, their death was inevitable, meaning I could dispose of him in a manner that looked like an accident. He would simply have fallen from his own ingeniously designed deck.

Three days later, Feldman was dead.

1962

I was headed for California—having worn out my welcome in upstate New York—by way of yet another bar fight. Still fresh into grappling with my soul over the death of my son and lashing out at anyone and everyone, I had decided to depart that state after reading a not-too flattering article about myself in the local newspaper titled "Troy Man Assaults Son of Shipping Magnate, Roland Hasting."

The cross-country bus ride from New York has not been uneventful. Now at a stop in Albuquerque, New Mexico, sitting at the bar of a local dive with $108 (my total net worth) in my pocket, I am reflecting on my next move when a surly-looking military-type pulls up a stool.

It is the beginning of a journey that can only end in death, which is somewhat appealing to me, as it is death that I am both running from and looking for!

We strike up a typical barroom conversation about the ups and downs of life. I find him easy to talk to. After several beers, I find myself telling him about the death of my son and my subsequent downward spiral to my current standing—sitting at a bar 1,300 miles from home with $108 in my pocket and a bus ticket to California, headed to see a school teacher I knew in New York, who is now living and working there in a town called Riverside.

He tells me that he already knows who I am and that he has been following my exploits since the day of my son's burial. He had been at the cemetery on the day of *Jimmy's* burial?

He never explained how he happened to be there, just that he witnessed my overwhelming sorrow and felt that I might be someone that would be of use in his line of work. He never mentioned what his line of work was, only that it paid *extremely* well and required an extremely rare type of individual: one who had the mental mindset that I *seemed* to possess.

I noticed the time and realized my bus was leaving in three minutes. I told him I had to leave immediately and started off my stool. He quickly handed me his card and said goodbye.

Once back on the road to California and comfortably seated in the very back of the bus, I took his card from my pocket. It simply read: THE KEEPER 1.

1982

Life is good. My identity has held strong for over ten years. It's looking like I may have truly achieved deep cover, even as I continue to carry out "deep black" assignments for my country.

I have managed to grow my auto leasing company into one of the largest in California. My relationship with Roxzanne ended after about two years in a drunken night of mistrust and stupidity—on my end, not hers. In a word, I "blew" it.

Some horses don't pull well in double harnesses.

Nonetheless, it seems I have somehow survived long enough to be in a mid-life crisis—would have bet against it! Lately, I find myself in a constant state of self-analysts. Seems I'm not too happy about not only having survived but thrived in an arena meant for an early grave.

The KEEPER keeps.

His name is J. Daniel Fasinelli.

He's a high-flying *financial wizard* based in Delmar, California, dating Delmar's mayor, Clancy Glover, and most recently voted "Mr. San Diego" by the *San Diego Magazine*.

Friday night finds me sitting at a table at a local Delmar steak house named Bully's West, with Fasinelli, Glover, and San Diego Mayor Ben Hedgefield. It seems Fasinelli is always looking for investors in his firm and guarantees a 25 to 50 percent yearly return on investment with a proven track record and some very influential investors and supporters, not the least of whom are the two mayors sitting at the table.

His pitch is virtually nonexistent. He says little and acts very much like the nerd he is rumored to be. Glover and Hedgefield, on the other hand, continuously extoll his financial accomplishments up to and including his most recent debut on the cover of San Diego's most prestigious magazine.

Given my nature, I am more interested in Clancy Glover's beauty and intellect than I am in handing $1 million over to Mr. Fasinelli. She is a natural blonde beauty with a professional demeanor and intelligence I find quite attractive. Turns out, she likes to party and enjoys her J&B scotch on the rocks with a twist of lime.

The two o'clock hour finds Clancy, Ben, and me looking for the after-party, while Fasinelli has already retired for the evening. It is agreed that my condo at the beach may be a perfect place to end the evening. We all decide to take separate cars, and as we exit the restaurant, Glover slips a small brown bottle into my hand. Let the party begin!

Somewhere around 4 a.m., Clancy and Ben leave. As I attempt to wind down off the cocaine, I light a joint and grab a cold beer. A knock on the door. It's Clancy. She has her high heels in her hand and a very sexy look on her face. I hold out my hand for hers and lead her into the bedroom. Let the games begin!

She is a very adroit lover—uninhibited and very romantic. I sense danger—beautiful, sexy, bright, wealthy, and powerful. She would be easy to fall in love with.

I vow to stay away from her. My instincts are well-honed, and I sense a very real danger, feeling that somehow, she is either connected to my past or detrimental to my future, which I have only recently started to acknowledge may actually exist.

Monday morning finds me mired in the chaotic world of running the largest independent leasing brokerage in the state of California. I thrive in its atmosphere—feeling alive and almost high on the action and excitement of out-negotiating the other guy and building a successful business. I feel at home in this world. For the first time since *Jimmy's* demise, I somehow have managed to use the word *home*. But the havoc and death I have unloaded on the world continue to haunt me day and night. Perhaps this is why I bury myself in work during the day and alcohol, drugs, and sex throughout the night. I am a man running from a past full of death, destruction, and sorrow, looking for something I am destined never to find: peace of mind.

My secretary hands me a hand-written message.

"This gentleman called a few minutes ago. I offered to put him through to you, but he insisted that I just hand you this message."

The KEEPER

1962

I arrived in Riverside, California, and was picked up at the bus station by Janet, the school teacher from New York. Had I not been in a complete state of rebellion and anger at the cards life had dealt me, I may have recognized then as I do now that she was a great lady.

I immediately obtained a job as a car salesman at the Riverside Auto Center. They gave me a brand new Mustang as a demo, and the party was on. Drugs, alcohol, sex, and danger were my way of life, and it did its job—kept me from thinking about the past as much as was possible.

A few weeks later, as I was walking around the pool table in a local Riverside strip club called Playtown, I reached into my back pocket for my comb, and a card came out with it. "The KEEPER1" reminded me of the dude at the bar in New Mexico. As I looked at the card, it suddenly came to me that it may be code, the letters signifying numbers: 8435337371.

Having ingested enough beer to be feeling both handsome and bulletproof, I proceeded to the phone booth in the corner and dialed the number.

"Hello, NewMex," was the greeting I received. "I see you finally figured it out; well done."

"So, what is this job you mentioned?" I said.

"There is a steak house there in Riverside on Magnolia Avenue called The Sire. Know it?" he said.

"I'll find it."

"Meet me there on Monday at 10:00 p.m. I'll be at the table in the corner by the fireplace."

And he hung up.

"Cocky bastard!" I thought.

Come Monday night, I walk into The Sire, a small, intimate steak house and lounge with a lot of heavy dark wood and sparse lighting, with paintings of famous racehorses framed in heavy mahogany decorating the walls, each lit individually by a small brass lamp.

As advertised, he is sitting at a corner table in the bar area close to the stone fireplace. I can't help but observe that he is seated in the chair in the corner. Wild Bill Hickok comes to mind.

As I approach the table, he stands up, shakes my hand, and addresses me as *Mr. NewMex*, not giving me his name.

"Mr. Keeper," I respond. And that would be the only name I would ever know him by.

He is drinking a Stoli's water over ice. The waitress comes over, and I order a bottle of Miller Lite with a chilled glass. *Don't pour it.*

The next thirty minutes would change my life *forever*!

When my beer arrives, and the waitress leaves, and he determines we cannot be overheard, he begins.

"Son, I am authorized by the United States government to recruit special operatives to carry out ominous, deep black operations known only at the highest level. There is a six-month probation program during which you will be trained and become proficient in all methods of subversion and termination. Your past will disappear *completely*, and you will be given a new identity. Only three will know of your existence: me, the president of the United States, and one other, who shall remain anonymous until such time he wishes to reveal himself to you.

"Having completed a minimum of ten successful terminations, you will be given the opportunity to continue at an annual salary of $500,000 cash, plus a "get out of jail free" card, or you will be released from service and free to live as you wish. Upon separation, you will be given $1 million in cash with the same "get out of jail free" card good for the rest of your life. We will watch over you and facilitate your disappearances and rebirths as needed to keep your true identity and your deep black deeds secret.

"You have twenty-four hours to decide. Whatever you decide, you are never to mention this conversation or the nature of its offer. If you do, you will be removed and terminated immediately along with whomever you told. If you accept, understand this, *it will never be over for you*, *NewMex*. This is a lifetime mission that will not end until your death—natural or otherwise. Do you understand?"

"I do, and I don't need twenty-four hours. When do we start?"

He smiled a knowing smile.

The Mission

It has been twenty-plus years and a myriad of successful terminations since I first spoke with the KEEPER, and now, another phone call. Knowing he is not the type to call and inquire how I'm doing, there was only one other option to consider: a call to duty, as I had never officially terminated my service and collected the $1 million separation pay. I was still collecting my $500,000 per year salary as I had been for years. I assumed I was about to be called into service in a big way.

Knowing the KEEPER did not partake in wasting time, I picked up the phone and called immediately. Three rings and then, "There's a bar in Ensenada, Mexico, called The 3rd Die. Know it?"

"I'll find it!"

"Meet me there in three days at 3 p.m., Pacific daylight time."
Click!

I smile. I've always admired his love of brevity. Three rings, three days, 3rd Die, 3 p.m.?

Don't forget about the third person? Was that the message? Was the third person going to be at The 3rd Die? Was there no longer a third person, or had the third person died or changed? Was I about to meet the third person?

The 3rd Die was a local dive bar located in the bowels of the city frequented by local cowboys, drug dealers, badasses, and whores. I had the feeling that this meeting included an opportunity for the KEEPER to assess whether or not I had maintained my earlier training and conditioning. It had been quite a few years. I was sure he was curious. I decided to drive to Ensenada a day early, get a room then check out the clientele at The 3rd Die.

A mystical winged warrior with sword in hand sits invisibly in the passenger's seat.

The logo on the sign was the Grim Reaper standing atop a pair of snake-eyed black dice. Not exactly a welcoming *sign*. It was a shithole full of assholes. It didn't take long for the assholes to start fucking with the gringo.

"Hey, gringo! What the fuck are you doing in my cantina?!"

Oh well, might as well get it over with.

I walked over to where the asshole was standing.

"You got a name, asshole? I like to know the names of people I'm about to fuck up."

His eyes betrayed his intention. As he reached behind his back for an eight-inch stiletto, I sent the heel of my right hand on a mission to his chin—*contact*—as his lower teeth said hello to his upper teeth, and blood and teeth spewed from his lips. I grabbed his greasy black hair and slammed his face into the top of my knee, immediately smashing his nose to the point of unrecognizable. As he was about to fall backward, I kicked him squarely in the balls. He was out of the game.

As another scar-faced, overweight Mexican came at me from the right, and what appeared to be a large cross-bred black guy was coming hard from the left, I quickly stepped aside, allowing them to meet in an awkward collision that left the Mexican unconscious and the breed dazed. I seized the opportunity to draw my .380 from my boot and put an end to round one. Pointing it in every direction at once, I requested that every mother fucker freeze and shut the fuck up, then threatened to shoot the next one that moved a hand or twitched a finger!

Just then, I noticed a sleeping vaquero in the corner remove the sombrero from over his face and stand up.

"Well done, *NewMex*, well done!"

The KEEPER! So much for a day early.

"This your idea a reentry exam?"

"It is. Okay, boys, get Pedro to the hospital and clean this place up!"

And with that, he escorted me outside to a waiting Humvee that sped off immediately after I entered it. The choice of a Humvee became apparent as we sped over rock-strewn roads that were more like gullies and firebreaks than actual roads. The enduro through the countryside was anything but smooth, and conversation was nonexistent.

Three hours later, we arrived at what appeared to be a Beverly Hills-style mansion, somehow transported to the high desert east of Ensenada.

A gentlemen's gentleman appeared at the twenty-foot-high front door as we approached, and speaking directly to the KEEPER, said, "Good evening, sir. The president is in the study."

As we entered the study, the president of the United States, Ronald Reagan, rose from the conference table at the far end of the room and approached us with his hand extended and a smile on his face—a cowboy hat on his head and western-style boots on his feet. *The boss lives.*

He greeted the KEEPER with a firm handshake and a stern but pleasant smile on his face. As for the KEEPER, his demeanor was one of strength and control with a let's-get-down-to-business attitude.

As the president turned to shake my hand, he said, "So, this our man called *NewMex*. A pleasure to meet you, sir, and thank you for the many services you have performed for your country. Please be seated, gentleman." A butler appeared with a Stoli's for the KEEPER, a Miller Lite for me, and a Jack Daniel's straight for the president.

For the next hour, I was briefed on the mission, a mission so black that the president of the United States had secretly flown all the way from Washington, DC, to another country before he would discuss its details.

The president, looking directly at me, began to speak.

"NewMex, twenty-some-odd years ago, your government chose to offer you an opportunity to carry out specific tasks for your country and earn a great deal of money doing so. You readily accepted this opportunity and have performed with precision and professionalism, the likes of which we have never experienced.

Specifically, you have not only accomplished all of your missions with the utmost efficiency, but you have demonstrated an ability to remain silent and sane, which is indeed your greatest accomplishment. It is with this in mind that we have chosen you for this mission. We believe you may be the only person in the *United States of America* capable of not only successfully executing the mission but never revealing that it ever happened.

"Again, it is with this in mind that I inform you that these United States are on the cusp of losing a full 30 percent-plus of their landmass, specifically the states of California, New Mexico, Utah, Arizona, Nevada, Colorado, and Texas—all because of one family living in Colton, California, and one family living in Mexico City, Mexico. These two families mounted a joint-historical excavation of a sacred Navajo burial ground in and around the town of Cave Creek, Arizona. This excavation resulted in the discovery of a 250-year-old land grant whose existence was previously unknown. This post-Inca document gives irrevocable and unequivocal ownership of seven southwestern states to the Valenzuela family of California and the Cortez family of Mexico City—both very wealthy and influential families in their own right.

"Should these two families exercise their right of possession, which without a doubt they will, our two countries will be tied up in litigation for years. And Mexican law states that 'under no circumstances shall any commerce or settlements be permitted on disputed lands during the litigation period!'

"Can you see the devastation this will bring to millions of families? Uprooted, homeless, forced to migrate to other states—causing a crushing effect on the economy, hundreds of thousands of businesses closed and abandoned, not to mention the looting and lawlessness that would occur. All in all, the horrific effects this would cause are unacceptable to the United States of America and its citizenry! This threat constitutes a national security emergency and invokes a declaration of war, allowing us to operate under the Articles of War.

"We are prepared, should it become our final option, to maintain possession by force, and we are well equipped militarily to do just that. However, when we factor the loss of lives on both sides—as many as 500,000 by some estimates—we look for another solution. And this is where you come in!

"Our investigations into both families have been extensive, as you might well imagine. The Valenzuela family consists of 187 members, including all relatives—men, women, and children. The Cortez family has another 219, for a total of 406 *individuals*. Or, if you choose to accept this mission, they would be referred to as *targets*."

"Are you with me, NewMex?"

"I am on the same page, Mr. President!"

The KEEPER spoke next.

"Normally, on a mission of this magnitude, we would operationalize two platoons from our best SEAL team to assist you; however, given the dark nature of this mission, the only individuals to know of its existence are in this room. President Reagan is here with us today to ensure that you realize through his own words and presence here that this mission, although very black and hard to justify, is both absolutely necessary and condoned at the very top of our government. We hope this will help you to decide to, once again, come to the aid of your country."

"I'm in. But how to put each and every member of these families and their friend together in one place at the same moment and then terminate them with a move that most assuredly must appear completely accidental. . . . Tough, very tough!"

"We have a plan."

"I thought you might."

"Both families' ancestries date back to the time of the Aztecs when families formed what were called 'Cauldrons.' All members within the Cauldrons were sworn to keep 'Cauldron Secrets,' under penalty of death. The Cauldrons of the Valenzuela and Cortez families are still in place to this day; therefore, the existence of the find, although known within the families, is, thus far, completely unknown to anyone else. For us, this is very fortuitous.

"It is also a practice within the Cauldrons that when the leaders of the families choose to go public with a 'Cauldron Secret' for reasons of financial or political gain, every member of the Cauldrons and their entire family must meet in secret to vote on the issue at hand. Even the youngest in the families have a vote, thereby assuring that *all* family members are present. As it turns out, this is, again, very fortunate for us and our mission.

"It will be your task to learn when and where this meeting is to take place and then remove all members through a method that, beyond all doubt, is an unfortunate yet tragic accident. We suggest perhaps a biochemical nerve agent.

"And by the way, NewMex, there is a $100 million bonus in this for you to be paid in cash eighteen months after the successful completion of the mission. We feel that it will take that long for us to determine if it was a *successful* mission. If what is sure to be an intensive investigation into this tragic *accident* has turned up nothing by then, the mission will then and only then be considered *successful*, even if we have to pull you out of character and reinvent you.

"The money will be placed in the same location in Jawbone Canyon, California, where you pick up your yearly payments. Having reviewed your abilities, judgment, and decisions over the years, we have complete faith that you will carry out the mission successfully. From this point on, there will be no need for future contact. You're on your own. However, we will pull you out if things go wrong."

ROXZANNE (REBOOT)

It was close to 11:00 p.m. when the Hummer dropped me off about a half a block short of The 3rd Die. I decided to drive a few blocks to the beach, having heard of a beach bar that had been converted into a tourist trap by a beautiful American woman (or so it was rumored), which was usually peppered with a spattering of local senoritas, hookers, and tourists—a much more pleasant environment than The 3rd Die.

After five beers and three shots of Baileys, I felt some of the tension from this afternoon's meeting and the possibility of a $100 million payday subside as memories of another mission slowly made the journey from the storage shed in the deepest and darkest recesses of my mind and began playing out all over again in my head. . . .

It was January 1963, at another deep black meeting and an assignment that would result in my being responsible for terminating over two hundred human beings—men, women, and children, in what would end up being referred to as the My Lai massacre.

I was deep in the Maicong Delta. I had arrived by gunboat to a make-shift army encampment temporarily erected in the dark purple and black jungle thicket. The smell of fire and vegetation, mixed with fog and smoke, filled the air.

I was greeted by Army General William "Bill" Westerman, and he described the mission. An entire village must be terminated, and I was to conduct the massacre.

Under his direct order, I was to arrange for and take part in the carnage—an incident that would receive worldwide coverage for "man's inhumanity to man," resulting in the conviction of Second LT William Calley as the perpetrator. I had some early regrets about that, but my conscience was later eased when then-President Nixon pardoned him. My most immediate role was to make my way to a small village in—

My thoughts were interrupted by a soft, familiar voice and a gentle whiff of Ciara perfume in the air.

"Of all the beach bars in all the beach towns in all the world. I can't believe you just walked into mine."

It was Roxzanne!

She was as beautiful and sexy as ever, maybe even more so. I could not help pulling her close and kissing her straight on the lips, and she returned the impulse with her tongue, gently touching mine. She wrapped her arms around my neck, squeezing me as if in an attempt to conjoin our bodies into one, letting me know clearly and simply that she was as happy to see me as I was to see her!

Must be on a buying trip, was my first rational thought after reluctantly removing my arms from around her waist. I felt a distant flame reignite, and from the look on her face and in her eyes—her eyes were like fingers feeling my thoughts, full of love and a bittersweet kind of sadness—so did she.

She accepted my offer to buy her a drink, and when she said, "Juan, another Miller Lite 'n' Baileys for the gentleman, and the usual for me," it hit me. By God, she's the beautiful American owner!

Reading my thoughts, she said, "Yes, it's my bar!"

There was very little reminiscing, only small talk about her bar and how she got there. There was a great deal of gentle touching back and forth and smiling deep into each other's eyes. A love, never given time to bloom, was what we both felt; although, I knew, as she did, that our paths were only crossing in the night and that a future together was very, very unlikely. After all, she was a street-hardened drug dealer, and I (my mind had trouble forming the words), I was an assassin!

During our long-ago two years together, I had introduced the art of Kikashi sex to Roxzanne, and although we had enjoyed engaging in its pleasures a few times, we had never achieved it. On this unbelievable night in the bedroom of her beach cottage by the sea, we did. After roughly forty-five minutes, cheating with only a couple of gentle touches to each other's faces, it happened. We both experienced massive organisms at the exact same moment, then fell together into each other's arms and stayed that way until the dawn. It was, without a doubt, one of the most incredible and beautiful moments in both our lives, igniting a flame that would burn for a lifetime.

It was a perfect next ten days, as I put thoughts of both my lease company and my impending assignment out of my mind and simply let love take its turn at controlling my life. It was a beautiful time—days full of sun and sand, basking in the serenity of the moment, and nights consumed with dining and dancing and walking on the beach with the pelicans—always ending in her bedroom by the sea, seeing and hearing only each other as the rest of the world seemed to fade and lose its purpose!

We were together there, as one, in love with the moment . . . both knowing the moment must end.

For me, it rivaled my time years ago in Hawaii with Katy—full of love and caring yet always with danger lurking. . . .

For Roxzanne, it was a pause full of happy moments and sad longing thoughts, a place where a hardened drug trafficker and saloon owner could let herself be trusting and soft. It was a time of love—to be short in time traveled yet everlasting in memory— filled with hours of gentle touches and stares into the very heart and soul of each other. We had both dived off the deep end without ever leaving the ground, both of us knowing yet refusing to admit that the water was thick with danger.

It was day ten for us, neither of us willing to allow our real lives to interfere with the beauty of the moment.

I was sitting at the bar while Roxzanne gave final instructions to a member of her staff in preparation for the sunset diners that were sure to arrive shortly.

"Hey, bitch!"

The words gave me the warning and caused me to reach for my .380. As I turned to the sound of his voice, I saw an overweight greasy looking, long-haired Mexican holding an Uzi at waste level. It was aimed directly at Roxzanne as she stood behind the bar. All my training came to bear. I screamed at Roxzanne to get down!

Pop, pop, pop! directly into his head, but not before he got off a short bust in Roxzanne's direction. He gasped and went limp, dead before he hit the floor.

Roxzanne stood behind the bar, a look of shock and love on her face. She knew she was hit. She knew she was dying. She was looking directly at me, saying good-bye and I love you.

I ran to her and caught her in my arms. As I held her, she looked directly into my heart, touched my soul, and said, "I love you," with her lips. I felt her last breath on my face. She was dead.

When the lights grow dim and the curtain is drawn, I will carry these ten days into eternity and beyond.

The drive up from Mexico was filled with tears I didn't know I was capable of shedding. Not since the death of my son had I shed even one tear. And now, I was drenched in them. Was I getting soft? Or was I ridding myself of the last bit of love I would ever feel?

I had gone down a road that is forbidden for a man like me; I had allowed myself to *actually* love with complete abandon and had immediately been charged the toll: Roxzanne's life and a large irreversible deep scar on what was left of my heart.

I don't ever want to love again until it's with you again. Wait for me, Roxzanne; we'll be together again. Not just yet, but soon. . . .

For the next few days, I lived in a fog, torn between self-pity and sorrow. Filling my days with drugs, hookers, and booze, I made short calls to the office to let them know I was still in charge.

By the fourth day, I knew I needed to get my shit together. My country was calling on me, and I was, above all, a patriot.

I decided to start with the Valenzuela family in Colton, California. I left my lease company in the capable hands of my manager, Jim Waters, and headed to Colton, disguised as a modern-day gold prospector. I figured this might afford me some justification if seen wondering on Valenzuela land or inquiring about their holdings in an effort to connect with a close family member or friend.

After securing a hotel room and asking around about abandoned old gold mines in the area, I found a shithole gin mill on the edge of town that looked like a place where locals might hang out: the La Cabana Saloon.

I ordered a bottle of Miller Lite and a cold glass. At the pool table next to the bar, I saw what I was looking for: a grubby-looking dude with a beard wearing a T-shirt that read "GOLD FEVER." I just knew he was my guy.

I put up my quarters and hoped that he would not notice that I was letting him win.

By the end of the third game, we were on a first-name basis. His name was Ben Larsen, and he was a prospector. And he knew the area. He said the Valenzuela family owned most of the land in and around Colton and allowed prospecting with permission in return for 25 percent of every claim.

By the time I left, I had the directions to the Valenzuela Estate.

The following day found me pulling my recently acquired '61 Chevy pickup up to the gate that guarded the walled-in Valenzuela Estate. Convincing the gatekeeper I was a prospector seeking a permit to prospect on Valenzuela land, I was shown through the gate and directed to a small office off to the right that looked to be a converted guest house. Inside was not what I expected. As opposed to some old-timer sucking on a pipe and looking like the Lost Dutchman, I felt like I had just walked into the backroom of a western version of a Tony Soprano saloon.

Two mustached vaqueros standing around an antique pool table looked at me like I was fresh meat, and a third—a white guy, looked like he had been fathered during a rough night out by John Gotti and a Vegas hooker named "Lucresha."

"Howdy, gentleman. Lookin' to do a little prospecting in this area. Understand from the local chatter that I need a permit."

"Why do you want to hunt gold on Valenzuela land?"

"Good as any. Besides, I heard that if a fella gets lucky, he might go home a rich man less 25 percent, of course."

"Those hands of yours don't look much like prospectors' hands; they look more like city slicker hands."

"It's only my second time out. I tried my luck last year in the Yuma, Arizona, area and kinda got hooked when I picked up some placer gold on the Kofa Mountain Range. Started doing a lot of research and decided on Valenzuela land."

"Alright, buddy, sign your name right here. Put down your name and address and driver's license number, and don't try to skim on the 25 percent. We'll find you if you do, and it won't be pleasant for you. Got it?"

Hell, I just might be in the backroom of a Tony Soprano saloon.

As I left through the gated entryway, I couldn't shake the feeling that the Valenzuela family was somehow tied to the Mexican mafia or maybe worse, which could bode well for the after story.

That night, I returned to the La Cabana Saloon hoping to run into my pool buddy Ben Larsen and then inquire about the local talent. Nothing like a good whore to clear the mind. A whore is a whore, but a *good* whore is one that makes you believe she is in love with you. How do you find a good whore? *$$$*

Tonight, I felt like believing someone was in love with me.

Ben was at the La Cabana Saloon. We shot some pool, drank some beers, and he agreed to point me in the right direction, as far as prospecting on the Valenzuela property went. He made an offer that we team up, which I quickly squashed, telling him I was too greedy to share. Due to the nature of my real mission, it was imperative I work alone.

Her name was Ellie. She was recommended as "a very high-priced hooker," and she was that—$1,000 a night. But as it turned out, she was worth it. She was not only a perfectionist when it came to sexual pleasures, but she had seemed absolutely enthralled with me, giving me her *private number* and asking if we could go out on a date together. She had me believing she was in love with me and that I was special. She was a "good whore." I knew I'd be calling her again and soon.

The next day found me making a trip to the Valenzuela estate. I positioned myself about a mile away and began my surveillance of the property. My state of the art Bushnell thermal rangefinder binoculars were the best money could buy. From a mile away, they literally put me in the living room of the estate. I searched for any clue that would lead me to a final decision on a method of termination. It was one of three (funny how that number keeps coming up) things I needed to carry out my mission. When 'n' where were the other two, and I have a strong feeling that my new drinking buddy Ben would somehow help lead me to both.

For now, my binoculars had me feeling like a voyeur as I observed what was a gorgeous young woman enter the interior courtyard for what looked to be a morning tanning session by the pool. Wait! By god! It was Ellie, the $1,000 a night whore. Things just got easier.

Turns out, she is a regular at the estate whenever the wife and kiddies are out of town.

Two weeks of surveillance and four more visits to Ellie yielded me the information I needed and found me back in San Diego.

The Furnace Creek Inn & Resort in Death Valley, California, was the meeting place, and *Christmas* week was the time.

CLANCY

Monday morning finds me back in the office at 5:15 a.m., wanting to check things over before any of the staff arrives. As I unlock the door to the offices, my proximity sense, a sixth sense that lets you know that someone else is in the immediate proximity without seeing or hearing them —which I had acquired in the jungles of Vietnam—goes into overtime. My .380 finds its way from my ankle to my hand as I flip on the light switch.

"The janitor let me in. He recognized me from the newspapers, and I assured him it was okay. Are you going to shoot me?"

It was Clancy, the Delmar mayor I had vowed to stay away from.

"I was disappointed when you didn't call me, Mr. Hawk! I find you quite charming and—"

"Why are you snooping around my offices at five o'clock in the morning?"

"Well, the truth is your name came across my desk recently in connection with an apparent drug deal gone wrong in Pacific

Beach a few years ago, so I decided to do a little investigating on my own."

She was slowly walking toward me with a very sexy look on her face. Displaying unmistakable body language—eyes barely open, head tilted slightly to the left while the tip of her tongue slowly moistened her parted lips—her body gently swayed from side to side as she rested her arms on my shoulders.

"You showing up and catching me might just be what I was hoping for."

Her arm went around my neck, her lips were on mine, and I was falling in love *again. Had I learned nothing from my recent affair with Roxzanne and the inevitable results?*

We made love on the sofa in my office for over an hour. My god! She was a great fuck and very, very beautiful. I was in trouble, apparently in more ways than one.

I managed to get her out of there before any of my employees arrived, proceeded with my day going over the sales and the books, making sure everyone and everything was ticking to the right time. All was well. Sales were good, profits were up, and I could not stop thinking about Clancy. My attraction to her was as strong as I had feared it would be if I saw her again, and my premonition of danger I had felt on that first night I had met her was proving to be correct.

What did she know, who exactly was she, and what was the deal with this Fasinelli guy? Ever since our meeting at Bully's West, my instincts had told me that he was not what he appeared to be.

We had agreed to meet that evening at the Old Ox, a steak house in Mission Valley just across the freeway from my offices.

As I sat at a high top table in the corner of the bar, I was juggling the dangers of what she had said about the "drug deal gone wrong" in Pacific Beach, knowing this was the deal with Roxzanne that had netted both the coke and the money. I couldn't help but smile and think, *gone wrong for whom*?

She came walking into the bar, scanning with a practiced and commanding presence that caught everyone's attention. She was *stunning* in every sense of the word. She was indeed everything I loved and wanted in a woman. Her eyes caught mine, and we both seemed to smile the same "I'm right here, babe" smile as both of our heads ticked slightly up.

We kissed hello as if we had been together for years. I was in dangerous waters, and I knew it. Falling for someone who was investigating me was dangerous enough, never mind who I really was and what I was involved with!

"So, you see me as a drug dealer?"

"No, at least not *only* a drug dealer. I see you as a man who is addicted to danger and beautiful women. A sloop, which matches the description of yours, and a beautiful dark-haired woman were observed at the scene of the shooting."

"Shooting, now, is it? The plot thickens."

She slid her stool closer to mine and looked at me in a way that put me on my guard. Her eyes said she was fascinated by me and that she wanted to get very intimate with me. My sense of self-protection said she was a very clever bitch with all the attributes to make a man turn into a schoolboy in her presence. The game's afoot.

That night, we made love on the bay. As we floated silently over placid waters, I could sense a bit of jealousy coming from the *LadyHawk* as she creaked and moaned in motionless seas. Clancy was beautiful in every way, and I was definitely attracted to her. However, it had been her suggestion to go midnight sailing on the bay—the scene of the crime and the getaway vehicle. *The irony was not lost on me.*

The game was definitely on, and another plate was spinning.

I did a quick mental inventory for any evidence that might connect me to "the drug deal gone wrong," as Clancy had named it. The shell casing from the 30.06 had gone overboard with the shot, and I had deposited the weapon in the ocean about a mile off the coast that night. The coke and the money went to Roxzanne, and Roxzanne was dead. As long as I didn't let my tongue trip me up, I was in good shape, and I needed to ease off of Clancy and forget about her. *Yeah, right.*

The Inn

I had about four months to plan the "mission" to prevent the devastation and death of hundreds of thousands of Americans and Mexicans. Sacrifice the few (406), thus save the masses. That was not only my justification for what I was about to do but "the way of it." I could not dispute the logic. At least, that's what my heart was telling my soul.

During these times, when heart and soul are struggling with each other, my mind always wanders back to my first mission. The one that was buried deep in the darkest canyons of my soul's soul. The one that could *never* be known or ever mentioned and should not even be remembered. The one that I needed to forget ever happened. The one that needed to stay buried deep in those canyons forever. As I struggled to push it back into the darkness of my soul, where it needed to rot and decay and disappear, I could smell the grass, hear the crowd, see the target, taste the fear, and feel the emotion of that moment. I was about to kill an earthly god, a person respected and loved by millions . . .

Stop! Done!

It was, again, locked away in the deepest, blackest canyons of my soul where it belonged, hopefully never to surface again.

The Furnace Creek Inn was perfect. In the middle of Death Valley, miles from anywhere, the resort had been built in the late 1920s by the Pacific Coast Borax Co. for the purpose of attracting tourists to the area. The resort has been expanded and improved upon over the years but never really caught on in popularity.

The families had obviously chosen it for its isolation, which, for my mission's purpose, could not be better.

I decided to don a retired elderly well-to-do gentleman's disguise and case the inn as soon as possible to get a lay of the land and look for a method to complete the mission. Given that all 406 souls must first be accounted for and then terminated simultaneously, *and* it must appear to be a freak accident, the task was not without difficulty.

The possibilities were only three: gas or poison or both.

I arrived at the inn late on a Friday afternoon, having made a reservation for a two-night stay. I was instantly impressed with the circa-1920s grandeur of the place. This, along with the very attentive staff, presented the distinct possibility of a quiet and pleasant weekend. Having surveyed my room, I gravitated to the bar, where I ordered Baileys on the rocks. A perfect disguise is one that is all-inclusive—dress, mannerisms, voice, movement— and free from redundant, everyday habits.

The resort itself was as I had previously thought it might be: *perfect* in every way. Isolated, old, lightly staffed, and, as luck would have it, heated and cooled by an old gas-powered system.

The piano player in the bar was singing Elton John's "Someone Saved My Life Tonight," which seemed to put me in mind of the ever-lovely Clancy Glover. She was very much the exact woman I was looking for mixed with an element of danger that I always seemed to attract somehow and enjoy. Having previously instructed myself to stay away from her, I now found myself ignoring my own advice.

I found it relatively easy to wander throughout the inn and inspect the ventilation system. With the place so lightly staffed, there was virtually no one to interrupt my walking directly into the room that housed the power grid for the resort. Knowing that, should I be discovered, I would simply resort to my typical "old-man who had wandered off the tourist path and ended up in the cellar" act.

The system appeared to be basic—several large air conditioning and heating units with a multitude of air ducts running in every direction. If an ample amount of powdered VX

nerve gas (a biochemical warfare agent) was placed inside each vent and the flames were to be extinguished on the burners and the gas still flowed pulling the VX along with it . . .? It could work.

Theoretically, all 406 souls, plus the staff, would die instantly. An explosion would follow, completely obliterating all evidence and leaving the ages to wonder and speculate on how such a tragic accident could have occurred.

Perfect!

A bit more exploration netted an outside rear door in the hotel (with no lock on it) leading directly to the maintenance room. Easy in, easy out. The plan was taking shape.

SAUSALITO

A black limousine with five occupants rolled slowly down the road—blurred, barely visible, viewed as if in a tunnel. A shot rings out, the smell of gunpowder and fresh-cut grass. Dead, deformed babies floating through the air—some with two heads, many with decayed faces. Sirens. Skeletons dressed as soldiers, the smell of death, and little coffins passing by.

I awoke covered in sweat, jerking straight up in bed. It was the third time in less than a week that I had had the same dream.

My leasing company was running itself with the help of my sales manager, Jim Waters, to the tune of about $100,000 net per month.

Eighteen years plus without compromising my cover, thanks mainly to my "death" in Hawaii and the continued excellent work of the KEEPER.

The KEEPER keeps.

Why the dreams now after all these years? *Perhaps all the years of secrecy and death were catching up to me.*

I rolled out of bed and checked the date on the wall calendar: December 2, about three weeks to my date with the total elimination of two families whose lineage dates back to the Inca Indians—all in the name of the preservation of the world dominance of the United States of America.

No problem. . . .

I felt a need to get away, maybe a trip to Sausalito in northern California.

I booked a bungalow at the Alto Mira Hotel on a hillside just above downtown Sausalito and decided to buy a new Corvette and slow roll the trip up, maybe stop in Carmel for a night.

As I rolled out of my gated underground garage in the early morning beach sunlight, I felt an internal warmth I had not felt in a very long time. The anticipation of the road trip up the ocean-hugging Highway 101 was at this moment overriding the planned destination. Perhaps the journey is the destination.

Twenty minutes later found me on the 101 coming down out of Torrey Pines, descending on the beach town of Cardiff-by-the-Sea. As hoped, I was finding the drive very exhilarating. My first destination was the Monterey-Carmel area—the home of John Steinbeck, Cannery Row, and Clint Eastwood.

About six hours up the coast.

Millions in off-shore bank accounts, an exquisite road machine, a beautiful day, my friend (the sea) on my left side, and an angel watching over me (the KEEPER). Why, then, was I feeling so anxious? I basically achieved everything I had set out to do and be.

Yet the sadness and anger that had overcome me in a cemetery in upstate New York so many years ago were constantly lurking just below the surface, refusing to let go of the soul it possessed.

As the Corvette rolled effortlessly over the sun-bleached California roads, and the all-consuming smell of the sea pleasured my senses, my mind began to wander as it sometimes does in solitary moments, bittersweetly, back through the journey that was my life, stopping briefly here and there in places by the roadside, both happy and sad, good times and bad.

The ever-present danger in this type of freelance mind traveling is that *the soul of a man* surfaces and gently forces the question, *who am I?*

And for me, there is only one answer, an answer that seems to both scare me and pleasure me simultaneously: shamefully admitting that I am not the altar boy I was in my youth while reveling in the knowledge that I fear no one, for *I am the bad guy*.

I am an assassin. A trained and accomplished killer of humans, possibly the best in the world. I take both pride and shame in this fact.

As I approach the town of Carmel-by-the-Sea, nestled on a hillside next to my friend the sea, I realize that I have driven straight through lunch and arrived at dinnertime.

Deciding to spend the night and resume my road trip in the morning, I checked into the Village Inn, a quaint yet upscale bed and breakfast just on the edge of town. Next, I made a reservation for one at my favorite corner table in one of my favorite restaurants in Carmel, The Flying Fish, a quaint, sub-level dining establishment with a great atmosphere and terrific food.

Nursing a third Miller Lite and a shot of Baileys Irish Cream following possibly the best double-grilled salmon and prime rib dinner I've ever had, I'm trying to decide whether or not to drive over to Cannery Row and hit a couple of hot spots in Monterey or get a good night's sleep, get up early, and make it over the Golden Gate Bridge by noon.

My mind wanders and searches for the first kill. The smell of grass and gun powder, sirens blaring, and suddenly, a hospital corridor, children all around—deformed, two heads, webbed hands and feet, no arms . . .

Is doing nothing to save a dying child the same as murder? *If so, my first kill was a child. Maybe that's why it's so easy for me to take human lives.*

I decide to turn in early.

And hope not to dream.

But as I'm leaving, I catch a look from a very attractive, well-dressed thirty-something blonde sitting at a table with a setting for two and a look on her face that says "join me if you dare". . . .

I dared.

"Am I late?"

"On the contrary, cowboy. You're right on time."

She's beautiful, she's available, and as it turns out, she's my kind of woman—hot, horny, and for sale. Five hundred for the night? I'm in!

Just after noon, the next day finds me crossing the Golden Gate Bridge into Sausalito.

I was feeling all the way up. She was a great piece of ass and great at her craft—fuck 'em, take their money, and leave.

Perfect!

But I thought she loved me.

Ha-ha.

She was just an okay whore.

It's always a pleasure to arrive at the Alto Mira. A short twisting driveway up the mountainside, overly ambitious porters greeting you as you approach, parking your car and seeing to your luggage, and a beautiful young lady at the reception desk? It works.

My suite is a circa 1920s, second-story bungalow perched on the hillside overlooking the bay—pleasing, pleasant, and calming. But I can't sit still as the deepest well in my soul begins to ripple and stir up a surging wave of overwhelming sadness.

It's Miller Time!

The Bar With No Name—my favorite gin mill in Sausalito. It's "two o'clock in the afternoon on a Saturday" kinda quiet. A middle-aged businessman in a suit nursing a scotch rocks and looking like he is screwing up his courage for a late afternoon sales presentation is standing at the bar. An old beach bum alcoholic is making love to a bottle of Budweiser and a shot of Jack at the far end of the bar, and a bartender who looks like he came with the building is gazing up at the TV.

I order a Miller Lite and grab a stool at the end of the bar next to the front window. The omnipresent bandstand sits empty with the tools of the entertainers' trade standing watch.

Two hours later finds me ordering my fifth beer and starting to catch an ever so familiar buzz when in walks an attractive, hippieish-looking blonde who somehow vaguely looks familiar.

And when the bartender says, "Hey, Nicki!" it clicks. It's Nicki Stevens, the singer with the Redwood Jack Band.

"Hey Bobbie," she responds as she pulls up a stool next to me, and he places a bottle of Miller Lite in front of her. *How fortuitous*.

She looks at me, raises her bottle, and says, "Here's to good beer."

I smile, tap my bottle to hers, and nod. "Yes, ma'am, and beautiful women!" I say, looking at her approvingly.

She looks me up and down and says, "Get him another beer, Bobbie; we got us a player in the house."

Thirty minutes and a couple of beers later find Nicki up on the stage strumming an acoustic guitar and singing a sad and haunting ballad about a love lost long ago. She is one step beyond cool, and I'm fascinated by her.

As the day wears on and a few other locals roll in, she returns to the bar and again sits on the stool next to me.

"So, who are you?" she asks.

The next three days were a whirlwind. I was in love again. She was a soul mate of sorts—cool and successful but with something lying just below the surface: a tortured soul.

I never did find out what it was that made her so happy and sad and cool. She was *of herself* and made no claims or excuses for her deep-seated sadness that maybe only another unsettled soul like me could see or feel.

We drank a lot of beer, snorted a lot of cocaine, partied, and made passionate love for three days—knowing without saying that we were kindred souls and, at the same time, that it was to be short-lived and not to be.

The drive back down to San Diego is pensive—my mind wandering between Nicki, who I am, and the deadly chore ahead. At the moment, I am truly a lost soul haunted by the past, colliding with the present, and torn by the future.

Never forget who you are, or, in this case, who you are not. Never get out of character. *Hell, I've been Tim Hawk for so long, I'm beginning to believe I'm him—dangerous!*

THE LAND GRANT

When the seas ahead are high 'n' fraught
with danger, change course!

I am within days of eliminating 406 men, women, and children in an effort to save hundreds of thousands of lives and prevent possibly the worst American disaster since the Civil War.

The end seems to justify the means.

Why, then, am I struggling with it—the dreams, the uneasiness I feel. Are they trying to tell me there is a better way? Possibly. *And I may have an idea what that better way is.*

Back to Colton . . . and Ellie . . . and the La Cabana.

Two days later finds me sitting at the bar in the La Cabana Saloon, '61 pickup parked out front. Once again, I'm in my prospecting gear nursing a Miller Lite and looking for a move that would net me the information I was looking for, i.e., where is this "world-changing, recently discovered land grant" being kept?

Destroy the grant. Save 406 souls and the United States of America!?

I'm not sure I'm thinking straight, but I feel the need to try.

Why In the world am I thinking about how to save lives when I have spent my entire life taking them?

I do believe my heart is now taking control of the battle with my soul.

Let yourself care, Mr. Hawk, before it's too late.

I cannot help but notice a rather well-groomed and tough-looking Mexican sitting at a corner table. An array of distressed and nervous-looking Mexicans keeps coming to his table with a beggar's look on their faces and five minutes later leaving the table with a smile.

I turn a bit too quickly to a slap on my back.

"Take it easy, fellow gold digger. It's just your old buddy Ben Larsen."

Why am I so jumpy?

"Hey, Ben Larsen. Good to see you."

Three Miller Lites and a game of 8 ball later, I've learned that the Mexican dude at the table is Tony Montoya, a local celebrity along the lines of a Jesse James (a *good* "bad guy").

According to Ben, he's heavily connected to a certain drug lord in Tijuana, Mexico. He's known locally as the unofficial "Mayor of Colton," taking care of his small Mexican community by granting favors and monetary gifts to the less fortunate on a regular and ongoing basis, leaving him somewhere between Jesse James and Don Corleone. It was my bet that a connection to the Valenzuela or Cortez families was not far from the surface.

"Ben, am I running a little paranoid, or does that 'Mayor of Colton' fella keep giving me the evil eye?"

"He doesn't cotton to too many gringos. Most likely suspects you're a cop of some sort. They're always bugging him, trying to bust him for one thing or another."

"You know him?"

"Just from being in here. He knows I'm not the law, so he's okay with me."

"Where does he get his money from?"

"He operates a small, used car lot across the street, but rumor has it he has his hands in everything from gold mining to heroin trafficking."

"Gold mining?"

"Yes, he's tight with the Valenzuela family."

Bingo!

The next day finds me on the "Mayor of Colton's" car lot.

I find myself liking Tony Montoya. He is a strong and amicable Hispanic American with a demeanor that says don't fuck with me! We hit it off well. I haggle with him over a five-year-old pickup truck on his lot that I have no intention of buying, rather using the time to establish a relationship with him, hopefully, in the end, leading to the info I'm seeking on the Valenzuela family.

Knowing he is heavily connected and will undoubtedly have my background investigated, I confess that my gold-digging is just a hobby and that I own and operate a successful auto leasing company in San Diego. He invites me to join him at the bar tonight for "drinks 'n' whatever," as he puts it.

Double bingo!

Whatever turns out to be *Ellie* (but I thought she loved only me) and her coworker, Bonny.

A night of drugs, sex, and booze ends with Tony telling me he's headed to San Diego in the morning for a one-day stop-over on his way to Mexico and suggests we have dinner tomorrow night at The Butcher Shop in Mission Valley. "The fish is on the hook."

The Butcher Shop is an infamous local steak house located on the bottom floor of the International Hotel in Mission Valley, not far from my offices. It's known to be a favorite of both notorious underworld figures and high-level law enforcement officials, sprinkled with a few "ladies of the evening" who find the adjoining hotel convenient.

My leasing company is doing well. Through all the bullshit, I have somehow elevated my company to the largest leasing brokerage in California.

Tony is sitting at the bar when I arrive at the Butcher Shop in Mission Valley. He is quite a character. With a forward right-leaning black fedora on his head, he's wearing a black leather jacket, black jeans, and cowboy boots. Sitting next to him is a younger-looking John Delorean look-alike, also with a black leather jacket, plus black, skin-tight driving gloves on his hands. Turns out it's Jerry Wiegert, owner of the Vector Manufacturing Company.

Tony introduces me to Jerry as a friend of his. *We're getting closer to the prize.* Wiegert is soliciting Tony to invest in his car company and has brought with him the only car he has produced so far: the Vector W2 prototype. It's sitting in the parking lot waiting for Tony to demo. And now me if I'm interested in investing.

The Vector is a high-performance supercar built to compete with Maserati, Bugatti, and Lamborghini—capable of speeds up to 230 mph. Five beers and an investment-sales pitch later, Wiegert and his driving gloves offer to take me on a demonstration ride, which Tony has already refused. I'm in. Let's go!

We hit the San Diego freeway at 135 mph coming off the on-ramp, and seconds later, we're weaving through—thankfully—light traffic at 190 mph. I am equally impressed by Wiegert's driving acumen as I am with the car. Weaving through traffic at 200 mph is not for the timid. His huge balls and nerves of steel help to seal the deal. As we exit an S-shaped off-ramp at 110 mph and the Vector hugs the road like glue, I commit to a $500,000 cash investment in return for 5 percent of the company and 5 million shares, when and if the company goes public.

I will lose my $500,000 in the end.

When we return to the Butcher Shop, Tony has arranged for a large corner booth that seats six. He is seated with three lovely young *ladies*. As we approach the table, he says, "Shall we dine, gentleman?"

This man knows how to live.

About halfway through the meal, I manage to interject my gold-mining ambitions on Valenzuela land. Tony, who has just downed his fifth shot of Tequila and is nursing his seventh beer, jumps right in and tells me to quit roaming all over the desert.

"I'll introduce you to Fernando Valenzuela the next time you're in Colton, and he'll point you in the right direction. Just give me a heads-up when you're coming."

I love it when a plan comes together.

Time is short. The Furnace Creek Inn meeting begins on December 21, ends on January 2. And today is December 5— roughly twenty days left in which to meet with Fernando Valenzuela and determine if my alternate plan to secure and destroy the land grant will work. If not, I must terminate the lives of 406 souls— men, women, and children—in the name of safeguarding the United States of America. I'm having trouble with that and have decided that if that's the way it goes, I must rethink my killing in the name of patriotism. My heart and soul seem tired of the war. They seem to be trying to forgive each other.

Fernando Valenzuela

Friday, December 8, I'm on my way to Colton in my '61 Chevy pickup. Having called ahead, Tony has arranged for me to meet Fernando Valenzuela at his hacienda. As it happens, he is in town to wrap up some business before the Furnace Creek gathering.

There is a chill in the December air only felt in the southwest desert—a chill I like to refer to as *cozy cold*—kind of like a bittersweet physical feeling.

As I enter the La Cabana Saloon, where I'm set to meet Tony, I order a Miller Lite, and my senses are immediately alerted by the bartender's nervousness. A quick look around gives me the answer: two of the thugs I encountered at the Valenzuela ranch claims filing office sit at a corner table, looking mean and angry and making everyone edgy. In walks Tony. He heads toward the table where the two thugs are seated and signals me to join him.

It turns out that Valenzuela could not make it, but the two goons turn out to be okay. One's named Richard and the other Edwardo. They have been with Valenzuela for fifteen years and know the property well. They point me in the direction where most of the placer gold has been taken, indicating a specific area where the family's 25 percent has brought in tens of millions over the years: the southeast sector. Maybe I should be more serious about this gold-mining ruse I am perpetrating. More importantly, for my purposes, they are quite specific about where I am *forbidden* to go.

Interesting.

We all four sit and drink and talk for hours.

Richard and Edwardo are tough guys with a perverted sense of humor. I actually enjoy their company.

Tony, also, is a very cool character. He casually mentions my investment with Wiegert and the Vector, seemingly impressed that I had invested twice what he had.

Jerry Wiegert had had a very profitable night.

"I'm having a little difficulty wrapping my head around why a guy with enough money to invest a half-million dollars on a *maybe* is wandering around the desert looking for gold," he said.

"Yeah," I reply, "I must admit, it started out as a sort of hobby, something to do in my spare time besides drink and fuck. But the more I get into it, the more it seems to be turning into an entrepreneurial undertaking. For example, the way Richard and Edwardo here talk about tens of millions in profit at Valenzuela's 25 percent fee. That translates to gold hunters taking hundreds of millions. And when I start hearing those kinds of numbers, I'm in! Ya know what I mean, Tony?"

"I get it," he replies, "but whatever you do, as these guys have already warned you, STAY THE FUCK AWAY FROM THE NORTHWEST QUADRANT MARKED WITH 'KEEP OUT' SIGNS. If you wander in there even by mistake, you're a dead man!"

"I get it, Tony, but what the fuck is so important about that particular piece of land? From what I saw when I went out gold hunting the last time, it looks like just raw desert to me."

"Well, Mr. Hawk, it may very well be 'just raw desert,' as you put it; however, we do not question Mr. Valenzuela. Period! You comprehender? *Amigo!*"

"I got it, loud and clear. Now, let's have another round."

My original plan had a contingency that if I didn't get what I wanted out of Valenzuela, I would call Ellie (the good whore), and while enjoying her pleasures, I would see if I could squeeze any more information from her.

Now, after experiencing Tony's curiosity about my motives and spending habits, I felt a need to strengthen his belief in my gold-hunting sincerity—given I had just been pointed to where the gold may be. I decided the best thing for me to do (in order to keep my true intentions hidden) was to head out to the Valenzuela Ranch and actually do some gold hunting.

The next day finds me wandering through the desert like any other fool with gold fever. I was hoping to impress whoever they had assigned to follow me that I was genuinely looking for gold. And after that conversation with the two goons yesterday, I might just actually be looking. At least, that's what I was making myself believe—more convincing to the observers that way.

Using my compass and my binoculars, I had mentally mapped out the lay of the land. The main house was located precisely in the center of the twenty thousand-acre ranch, dividing each sector into approximately five thousand acres, or just short of eight square miles—the main house being at the edge of each sector.

Appearing to be gold hunting, I wandered to within two miles of the main house and used my binoculars to scan the horizon, taking care not to hesitate as I moved across the northwest sector. Even without hesitating, I could see that a small, raised area about a mile away from the ranch house was both heavily fenced and guarded—most likely a vault of some kind buried within the small rise holding the most-prized treasures of the Valenzuela family. And maybe, just maybe . . . the land grant.

Seeing what I needed to see, I called it a day and drove to La Cabana for a cold beer.

As I downed my fourth Miller Lite and searched my mind for answers, I began to realize that by veering from the KEEPER's plan, I was risking the entire operation. If I were to attempt to retrieve the grant and I missed it, we were done for. If Valenzuela knew someone was after the grant, he would surely cancel the Furnace Creek meeting. Not to mention the KEEPER. He had learned to rely on my judgment over the years and trusted I would stick to the plan and execute it flawlessly. He and the president had most likely already considered destroying the grant and arrived at the place where I was now, months ago. I was wasting my time with this foolishness!

I was either getting old or weak, and I cannot tolerate the thought of either. However, I did need to verify that the grant itself would be at the meeting to justify that not all my most recent chasing around the desert had been in vain. I decided to stick to my plan to see Ellie and find out what she knew.

Having learned from Ellie that Valenzuela had secured an armored vehicle for Christmas week, I baited her into whining about how pissed off she was that Fernando was on the phone with the armored truck company explaining that the only cargo they would be guarding was a locked briefcase, while she knelt between his legs seeing to his need for sexual stimulation.

I was now back in San Diego with only ten days to set up the Furnace Creek *incident*.

1962

The hospital ward was a horror show!

A three-year-old little girl with webbed, duck-like hands and feet walked up to him, then a four-year-old with a third of his head missing, a three-year-old with two heads, ten or twelve other children with a variety of deformities from no arms, to no legs, to no mouth, to three ears, to three legs, to no nose, and anything and everything else you have never dared to imagine.

This was St. Catherine's Hospital in Albany, New York—a haven for the unfortunate babies who have had the misfortune of being born into the outside edge of life, mostly unwanted for their abnormalities.

A sadness, coupled with dread and a shocking combination of fear and vengeance, shook the eighteen-year-old boy—who had most recently become the father of just such a child—to the very bottom of his soul. His heart split in half along the way, leaving a wound that would never heal.

He was being given a tour of "our facility" by the hospital director, intended to encourage him to bring his first child, a son, to the hospital. He turned and left the hospital ward, refusing to accept what he had just seen.

Two Weeks Earlier

"You have a son," said the doctor as he entered the hospital waiting room. "However, he has a large blister on his back. Otherwise, he is quite healthy."

The boy was taken aback a bit, not quite sure whether what he had just been told was a little problem or a big problem.

"We'll be running some tests to determine what it is. It will take a few days."

"Will he be alright?" asked the boy.

"He'll live," deadpanned the doctor.

Now in the recovery room, the child-father looked to his eighteen-year-old child-bride as tears filled her eyes. He comforted and hugged her as he mouthed the words he did not fully believe, "It's okay, baby. I'm sure he'll be just fine."

Four days later, the doctor informed the parents that their son had spina bifida—a debilitating disease resulting from the backbone not fully forming around the spinal cord, causing lower-body paralyzation and irreversible brain damage. There is no cure. Babies with spina bifida may live a year or twenty years with proper medical treatment, would be wheelchair-bound, and would suffer from medium to severe retardation. Or "leave it in God's hands," as parents and priests would hint at. In other words, just put him in St. Catherine's Hospital and do not treat the disease. He would most likely die within a year.

This was the choice given to an eighteen-year-old father.

Parents said, "Leave it in God's hands, or you will spend all of your money and the best years of your life having to care for him. You are so young with a full life ahead of you. You don't want to burden yourself with this. *Let him die.*

Priests said, "There are hospitals that can take care of him and wheelchair basketball leagues if he lives into his teens, but it's *your* decision. If you're not willing to accept this burden that has been laid upon you, no one will blame you for leaving it in God's hands. If you do so, St. Catherine's will see to it that he feels no pain. He will most likely become deformed, possibly growing a second head, and will die within a year."

Is not helping your child to live the same as killing him?

The young father was assured that it is not— and pushed ever so steadily in that direction by all.

Seven months later, "Jimmy" was dead.

THE WAKE

The father had visited his son for the first couple of months but could no longer watch his son slowly dying as he began to grow a second head from the right side of his neck. The mother and the maternal grandmother would continue to visit the child until his death. The paternal grandparents spoke of the child only in whispers.

The wake was, of course, a closed-casket affair ordered by the father, who wanted to remember his son as a beautiful child. This was not to be. The maternal grandmother walked in as the young father was kneeling alongside the gold-trimmed miniature white coffin.

"Why is the coffin closed?" she barked. "I want to see him one last time."

"Absolutely not," the father said. The grandmother pushed the lid of the coffin open, causing the young father to glimpse the body before he could close the lid.

It was an image that would burn itself into the very soul of the young father forever. The body, clad in a ruffled white dress, could not be seen. The heads, however, were completely visible and horribly shocking—a death-gray, zombie-like skeletal face with sunken black eyes and what appeared to be a second head protruding from his neck.

The father slammed the lid, scolded the grandmother, and left the room. The image branded into his soul, along with the question, *why did I let my son die like this when there was a clear path to give him life—even if it was only for a few years*? Had the young father slowly murdered his own son, or was it all God's doing? Was his vengeance to be directed at God or himself?

The LadyHawk

A black limo, the smell of fresh-cut grass, a gunshot rings out, sirens screeching, dead bodies with two heads, small white gold-trimmed coffin, skeletal-like zombie soldiers in Vietnamese military uniforms, four winged warrior spirits on horseback riding through the jungle mist.

The dream again—always the same. . . .

With ten days to go, I got no time for this shit. Fuck what the clock says. "It's Miller Time!"

My lease company, with the able assistance of Jim Waters, seems to be running itself with 90 percent of our customers being upscale Southern California residents who like being catered to. They supply a steady stream of useful contacts, and all their personal information (including their tax returns—provided to us to qualify for their auto lease) accumulates in my personal files—mayors, lawyers, judges, politicians, sports figures, performers, etc., etc.

I have more control over the rich and powerful of San Diego and the surrounding communities than they would care to imagine. We now have offices in Encinitas and Rancho Santa Fe, as well as our original Mission Valley location. All is well!

It's Friday night. On Sunday, I plan on heading back to the Furnace Creek Inn for one more look around to ensure that my plan to place the VX nerve gas into the vents, turn off all the pilot lights on all the furnaces, and deactivate the automatic shutoffs will accomplish my mission.

Thoughts of Roxzanne seem to be ever-present—now presenting themselves as flashes of bittersweet memories with a strange yet beautiful sadness that somehow hurts in my heart and brings pleasure to my soul.

Day Five Of Ten

On the fifth night of our ten days together, Roxzanne gently asked, "Who are you, really? My female intuition tells me there is much more to "Tim Hawk" than just "Tim Hawk.""

I stared into her eyes and saw the fear she felt asking the question, not knowing whether or not she really wanted to know the answer.

It was never harder to stay in character.

I smiled at the tenderness of her question, took her face in my hands, kissed her ever so lightly on the lips, and said the words I had not spoken *and meant* for twenty years: "I love you."

"Thank you. I love you too," she said, returning my kiss as her arms went around my neck. We pulled each other closer.

"Hold on tight, babe. It's going to be one hell of a ride," I said as she melted into my arms.

"Whatever is has already been" (Ecclesiastes 3:15, NIV).

That ride is over. *Come on, Tim Hawk, get your shit together and move on....*

I decide to take the *LadyHawk* out and go bar-hopping on the bay. I board her in Quivira Basin, where I had left her a week before to have her barnacles removed and to be fully detailed inside and out and decide that the Barefoot Lounge on Paradise Island will be my first stop. I motor out of the basin making a starboard turn into the jetty, cruise under the bridge, and turn slightly to port as the *LadyHawk* glides effortlessly into the glass-like waters of Sail Bay.

The dock lights of Paradise Island and the Barefoot Lounge show themselves just ahead off the starboard bow. I notice a slight breeze coming out of the northwest off the port stern and decide on a change of plans. I raise the mainsail and shut down the motor. Grabbing a Miller Lite from the fridge, I light a joint and proceed to sail silently along the moonlit shores of the bay— alone again with my friend the sea.

Apparently, I am not quite ready to let her go. The solitude of the bay seems to have opened a portal, and Roxzanne stepped through it.

A centuries-old cemetery that sits next to a tiny fishing village about twenty-five miles south of Ensenada, Mexico, is where I had laid her to rest, knowing that she had no family—and she was wanted by the law in the United States. *Let them keep looking.* I know she would have loved that!

There stands a rusted and badly in-need-of-repair iron gate to guide you in—no walls, and maybe forty or fifty headstones worn down by centuries of salt-dampened winds, barely visible in the deep weeds and trees that live on a slope next to the sea.

With the help of the villagers, I lowered her into the ground there. She will love listening to the waves breaking on the shore and the sound of the seagulls overhead. And maybe, just maybe, the pelicans would come to visit her. She loved the pelicans.

A pelican glides silently overhead.

Two hours pass as the *LadyHawk* circles the bay. She moans and creeks—perhaps longing for open water where she can soar under full sail, jib flying high and bowed to its limit, mainsail stretched tight for maximum speed and performance, streaking over the rolling seas as if she commands them.

Not tonight, my Lady, not tonight. But soon. I promise. . . .

The soft glow of the dock lights on Paradise Island appears once again, this time off the port bow. A row of tiny cottages lines the beach next to the L-shaped dock, and lush green gardens, ponds, and waterfalls surround the patio of the Barefoot Lounge just beyond the glow of the lights. I accept the invitation and head for the dock—lowering the mainsail, letting it fall gently to the deck, and timing the docking perfectly as the *LadyHawk* glides to a stop. I step from the helm onto wooden planks of the dock and secure her to its cleats, secure the mainsail to the boom, and step back to admire her beauty at rest.

The lounge is semi-crowded with late diners. I pull up a stool at the bar and scan the room. The bartender, who's kinda hot in an overly tanned, naturally blonde kinda way, says, "Miller Lite and a shot of Baileys, Mr. Hawk?"

"You have me at a disadvantage, miss . . .?"

"I'm terribly sorry, Mr. Hawk. Micki, Micki Stevens. My day job is at Mariners Shipyard over in Quivira Basin. I worked on the *LadyHawk* this week. She's such a beautiful sloop. I saw her pull up just now and figured you must be the Tim Hawk listed on the invoice. I saw the Miller Lite in the fridge 'n' the Baileys in the side rack when I helped detail her, so when I saw you, two and two seemed to make four. Is my math correct, or would you prefer something else?"

"No, your math is absolutely correct, Micki."

As Micki smiles and turns to retrieve my drinks, and I am quietly enjoying watching her walk away, a tap on the shoulder. It's Clancy, looking more beautiful than ever but with a difference: her body language is projecting a definite lack of her usual over-the-top confidence in herself. She actually seems a bit uncomfortable in her skin, if not even distraught.

"Tim, can you join Ben and me at our table for a few minutes? We would like to speak with you in private."

"Sure, I'll be right there. Give me five minutes."

She looks from me to Micki, who is just now bringing my order, smiles a knowing smile, nods, and returns to her table. Micki sets my Baileys and beer on the bar.

"Thank you, Micki. You live near here?"

"Yeah, next to the Catamaran on the other side of the bay with three of my girlfriends."

"Cool. I'm going to have a quick meeting with a couple of friends over there. What time does your shift end?"

"One o'clock in the morning. Why?"

"Great! I'll only be a few minutes. Could you save my seat here till I come back? I'm kind of enjoying talking with you. I love the sound of your voice; it's very cool."

"Of course I can, and thank you for the compliment. My friends say I sound like I have a cold all the time."

"Your friends are most likely envious. The fact is your voice is very sexy."

I slide a $50 bill across the bar and tell her, "Thank you."

She looks up, surprised, and asks, "Did you want to close out your tab?"

"No," I respond, "just put that in your tip jar, and I'll be back."

A quick look at my watch tells me it's 11:35 p.m. Perfect!

Clancy and Ben are looking nervous and anxious as I pull up a chair at their patio table.

"You two don't look so good. Did someone die?"

"Haven't you been watching the TV or reading the newspapers?" Ben asks.

"No, I've been out of the country for a bit. What's happening?"

"It's Jerry and the business!" Clancy chimes in with tears in her eyes. "They are saying that the whole thing was a Ponzi scheme! It was all a scam. They have arrested him, and now they are looking at me because I'm his partner and live-in girlfriend. All that really happened is that Jerry made a couple of disastrous stock trades. Word got out, and people started taking their money out, and the next thing you know, our checks are bouncing, and then everything collapsed!"

I smile inside and thank my instincts for their guidance in my having known something was not right with 25 to 50 percent yearly gains.

The silence that follows is overwhelmingly uncomfortable. Both Ben and Clancy are staring at me as if I were expected to fix it, or at the very least, say something brilliant. So I do.

"Wow!" I say. "Looks like you guys are fucked."

Just then, I feel a tap on the shoulder. It's Micki. "I'm sorry to interrupt, Mr. Hawk, but the bar is full and . . ."

"I get it, Micki, I'll be right there," I say as I get up and excuse myself from Clancy and Ben, saying, "We'll talk later. Good luck."

As I approach the bar and pull up my stool, Micki is smiling a smile that is very inviting. I say, "Thank you, Micki. You might not realize it, but you just saved me. It's 12:20 a.m. You're off at 1:00 a.m.?"

"Yes, I am, Mr. Hawk. Why do you keep asking me that?"

"Tim! Please call me, Tim."

"Okay, Tim. So, why?"

"Well, seeing as you live here on the bay, I thought perhaps you might like to have a drink with me on the *LadyHawk* when you get off, and I could introduce you to her properly as we sail around the bay for a bit. Then, I could drop you off on the beach in front of your house, yeah?"

Micki looks directly into my eyes for about fifteen seconds and then says, "I'd like that very much, Tim, but can I trust you?"

"No, absolutely not! You see, I find your voice and your appearance and your personality so very, very pleasing that I cannot say that it will go exactly that way. However, I can tell you that I am a businessman and a gentleman, and if you resist any advances I might make, I will respect your wishes."

She responds, smiling a very sexy smile. "In that case, *Mr. Hawk*, I will accept your invitation to formally meet the *LadyHawk* and trust that you are who you seem to be."

I kinda wish she had not said it quite that way!

I nod, lift my shot of Baileys in the form of a toast, "Hit me again, Micki!"

Not wanting to leave Clancy and Ben in a pool of blood, I leave my keys and my shot of Baileys on the bar, take my beer, and head back over to their table. I am quite curious about how they could go down so quickly when they had all the appearances of having been rolling in hundreds of millions of dollars.

As I approach Ben and Clancy, I notice that they have selected the patio table closest to the waterfall—the soothing sound of the water drowning out any conversation coming from their table. Looks like they are running a little paranoid, as well they should be. If what they have told me so far is correct, they are most likely under surveillance. I need to be cautious not to get dragged into the cesspool they are now swimming in.

I pull up a chair, turning it around so that my arms are resting on the back of the chair.

"How did you guys get into this mess? Did you know what Fasinelli was doing when he made the 'couple of bad trades,' as you put it? Seems to me he would have had to risk the entire operation—hundreds of millions in the stock market to cause a collapse."

"No, I didn't know. But apparently, that is what he did, an all-or-nothing kind of move. Stupid!" says Clancy.

"As for Ben, he is not part of the business; he is being accused of accepting illegal campaign contributions from our firm."

"Christ Clancy. You're both mayors. Can you not slow this thing down and get control of it?"

"No, we tried to do some damage control, only to find out we are both under investigation, and recall petitions are circulating on both of us."

"Goddamn!" I say as I get up. "I've got a friend I have to get back to. Let me know if there is anything I can do."

Ignorant, I think, as I leave the table before they can answer. I have no use for people who play checkers on the dark side. It's chess out here, not checkers.

Well, I guess the "shooting-on-the-bay" thing has been put to bed! As I head back to Micki, I notice a guy at the other end of the bar with a suit and tie on in a beach bar on a Friday night. The suit, coupled with the bulge under his jacket, spells cop.

As I reclaim my bar stool and smile at Micki while she is announcing last call, I notice another cop sitting by himself at a table—same outfit, suit, tie, bulge.

From the way they are eyeballing Clancy and Ben, I'm guessing they are not here on surveillance. One cop does surveillance. It takes two to make an arrest—most likely it's Clancy, as Ben's illegal campaign contributions crime is not a "two detectives in a bayside restaurant at one o'clock in the morning" type of offense.

Apparently, when Clancy said, "Now they're looking at me," she misspoke; they were looking *for* her! And now they had found her and, most likely, they would follow her out when she leaves and make the arrest. My guess is that there are a couple of patrol cars out front to assist in the arrest. I would have thought that she was smarter than this, but she is just a dumb bitch trying to play in the big leagues.

As I'm going to be waiting for Micki to end her shift and help close, it looks like I'm going to witness a little excitement. And I'm always ready for a little, or a lot, of excitement.

I sip my Baileys and drink my beer and start to wonder just how this will go down.

Clancy is clearly in a paranoid and neurotic state of mind—that, coupled with the several glasses of wine I have watched her consume and her recent *fall from grace*, could just make for an unpredictable reaction when they try to arrest her.

It's one o'clock in the morning. Ben and Clancy get up to leave. The two detectives converge on them immediately, not waiting for them to go outside. I watch Clancy as she sees them coming—badges in hand, jackets unbuttoned, hands on their guns. She reaches into her purse and pulls her government-issue .45 Automatic, and . . . *Pop!* One detective is down!

Jesus Christ! I knew she was in a paranoid state, but I *did not* see that coming!

The second detective puts a bullet in Clancy's neck. Blood begins pouring out everywhere. It's a terminal wound, one that will kill her within minutes. I refrain from pulling my .380 as it appears to be over. Ben drops to his knees and puts his hands behind his head, screaming, "Don't shoot, don't shoot!" Four uniformed officers come bursting through the door, guns drawn, pointing in every direction.

Employees and diners are in shock, although I sense that Micki is way too calm for this to have been her first rodeo. The few customers that were just about to leave are asked to stay, including myself and the staff, so that they can take our statements.

Clancy, beautiful even in death, lies in a large pool of blood as a result of a direct hit to her jugular vein.

The detective will go through a great deal of rehab, but he will live.

Ben ends up at the wrong end of the recall, beats the acceptance of illegal campaign contributions charges, goes back to surfing, and becomes a talk jock on local radio.

J. Daniel Fasinelli is sentenced to twenty-two years in a federal penitentiary. He is released after serving twelve of the twenty-two years.

It's 2:45 a.m. when Micki and I are cleared to leave.

We walk slowly out the door and onto to dock.

"Well, that was interesting," she states.

"To say the least," I respond.

The *LadyHawk* sits beckoning at her mooring.

We both seem equally mesmerized by her grace.

She is strong in her beauty, having an aura of both predator and prey—beauty and strength.

"Well? Are you going to introduce me to her? She looks like she wants to meet me. I think we could be friends."

We will spend the night anchored about a hundred yards offshore in front of her home. She is an interesting young lady. In the end, it was a one-nighter. I remain curious as to why she was so calm in the face of danger and death.

TEN-DAY COUNTDOWN

Sunday evening finds me checking in at the Furnace Creek Inn—this time disguised as a wealthy old cowboy—complete with hat, wig, turquoise belt buckle, full beard, silver-handled cane, high-dollar boots 'n' jeans, and more.

I cannot help but appreciate the beauty of the place—a combination of western-style, Hollywood-opulent furnishings inside, an eighteenth-century California mission outside—sitting right in the middle of the most desolate place on earth: Death Valley!

What a shame it is to destroy it. So much elegance and history. It's this or a war with Mexico over ownership of seven of our states.

No contest.

I have my luggage sent to my room and head for the bar. As I hobble into the bar, dragging my feet and leaning on my cane, who should be sitting at a corner table in the lounge? Tony Montoya and Valenzuela's two goons Richard and Edwardo.

I proceed to the far end of the bar and order a Jack Daniel's neat and a bottle of Coors beer in my well-practiced and perfected west-Texas, old man's drawl (distancing myself in every move and action from Tim Hawk). Maintaining my wealthy old eccentric cowboy demeanor, I down the shot in one swallow and sigh loudly before lifting the bottle of Coors and chugging it in one move. Slamming the bottle back on the bar, I burp loudly and follow with a large sigh of approval of myself. After peeling off a twenty from a large wad of bills, I throw it on the bar and tip my hat to the bartender before turning and hobbling off to my room.

It is most effective when hiding to do so in plain sight.

Valenzuela's security team, not surprisingly including Tony, has arrived early to thoroughly case the entire inn for any possible interruptions or dangers to either the Valenzuela or the Cortez families.

I had miscalculated their arrival, thinking they would arrive about five days ahead of the meeting, not ten. No matter. If I can't outsmart these assholes, I need to retire into obscurity and take up the rocking chair!

As I turn the key to my room, #33, the KEEPER comes to mind. What is all this *three* shit? What am I missing?

While pushing the door open, my proximity sense turns *red*. Someone's in the room; however, I do not sense danger. I pull my .380 anyway, hesitating behind the door.

Suddenly, I hear a familiar voice.

"Come on in, NewMex. Glad to see that your sixth sense is still functioning well."

It's *the KEEPER*. Christ, who isn't here?

"With all due respect, sir, I work alone. Remember 'you're on your own?'"

"I do, NewMex. However, when I heard that the Valenzuela security team had arrived ten days ahead of the meeting of the Cauldrons, I thought perhaps you could use a little assist. Great disguise, by the way. I saw that old man in the bar and did not realize it was you.

"Whether or not you would like or need some assistance here, I'll seize the opportunity to update you on what we have uncovered concerning the Valenzuela and Cortez families. I am assuming you have already realized their connection to the Mexican Mafia. What you may not know is that they *are* the Mexican Mafia.

"They are the overlords of all the cartels in Mexico—the Guadalajara cartel on down. They rule the roost, so let your mind wrap around what is now at stake here. Not only are we saving a half million lives and 30 percent of the United States, but we are also cutting off the head of the Mexican mafia! So the importance of the success of this mission has doubled, thus my presence. You good with it?"

"I'm good."

"How can I help? You need me to do anything?"

"Maybe. I'm a bit concerned about my connection for the nerve gas. If I use him, I'm forced to terminate him. He's been a great source for me over the years, and I most likely will need his services in the future."

"What are you using?"

"A powdered version of VX."

"The exact amount needed will be buried in the desert directly behind the maintenance door to the inn. I'll feed you the coordinates as soon as it's done."

"Next?"

"Media coverage connecting the Valenzuela and Cortez families directly to the Mexican mafia, including Tony and his goons."

"Already set to go."

"One more thing."

"Name it!"

"Tim Hawk will be a registered guest here at the inn that night. He will die in the explosion—authorities need to find an identifiable body—and I'll need all the necessary backup for a new start."

"Perfect! When you supply me with the name and location, I'll handle the rest."

"The name is Rick Hawk, my long-lost brother, who will inherit my entire estate and take up where I left off in San Diego. Can you arrange all the backup for a move like that?"

"A bit ballsy and not without difficulty. Consider it done. Anything else?"

"No, that's it!"

"I'll say this for you, NewMex, you haven't lost a beat. You're the best I have ever had the pleasure of working with. You have mastered your craft! Your country thanks you, your president thanks you, and I thank you for the services you have performed and continue to perform for your country."

"Thank you for that, sir. I have one question for you. What is it with all this *three* shit?

The KEEPER smiles.

"In all these years, NewMex, have you never wondered who is the 'one other' who has knowledge of your existence as a deep black operative?"

"Some," I respond, "but not enough to keep me up at night. Why?" I ask.

"Perhaps, as he would be number three to know of your deeds, he is attempting to tickle your curiosity? You see, twenty years ago, we would have never imagined that any *mere mortal* could have performed at the level you have. Although, after the thoroughness and precision you displayed on your first mind-bending kill in the early '60s (the unmentionable deep secret), we did suspect that you had the courage and strength of character to achieve greatness, as indeed you have done.

"Well, thank you for all the accolades, sir, but now my curiosity is peaked. Who the fuck is this mysterious third person?"

"No one ever said there was a third *person*!" he said as he left the room.

"What?!"

Four invisible mystical winged warriors enter as the KEEPER departs.

The next day finds Colonel Jackson Pickens (the name I registered under) hobbling about the grounds of the Inn, seemingly aimlessly, stopping by the bar every hour or so for his not-so-silent Coors and Jack regiment and becoming increasingly wobbly with each visit. This entire ruse has been a setup to allow me to "accidentally" wander into the maintenance area. With Tony's security team continually prowling the grounds, I need to appear harmless and lost in the event they happen upon me while I'm there.

Timing, as usual, is everything. Around 4:45 p.m., I notice that all three members of the security team have wandered into the bar. Taking advantage of this good fortune, I perform the Coors-and-Jack act again and wander off mumbling and wobbling, keeping Tony and company in my sights. Once outside, I reach the back door of the maintenance room, verifying once again that it is not locked. I slide inside.

A mystical winged spirit armed with what appears to be a trumpet takes up a position in front of the door—invisible to all...

The ventilation system is indeed perfect for successfully completing the mission—old and basic with vents spreading out in all directions from several feeder tubes, which, when filled with VX, will equally distribute the deadly poison throughout the entire building. I will simply need to catch the system in idle mode, turn it off, input VX, disable the pilot lights, turn the system back on, and get out quickly. I'll immediately remove myself from the danger perimeter using a high-powered dirt bike hidden in the desert brush not far from my exit position.

Return To Glorietta Bay

1975

The year 1975 finds me back at Glorietta Bay, this time sailing the *LadyHawk* after having skirted the kelp beds off Point Loma, cruising through San Diego Bay, sliding under the Coronado Bridge, and rounding the golf course. We are slowly approaching the center of the bay.

It is absolutely picture-perfect—the water as smooth as glass, the Chart House restaurant, our ultimate destination overshadowed across the roadway by the Hotel Del Coronado on our port side, the Glorietta Bay Yacht Club off the bow, and the Coronado Golf Course to the starboard.

Her name is Linda, and she is a twenty-six-year-old, hard-body La Jolla hairstylist—my hairstylist. When she offers me a glass of wine and a *line* on my third appointment with her and mentions that she has a passion for sailing and loves the sea, it's game on!

She is very cool and possesses a perfectly flawless body. Search as I may over the last few days, I cannot find so much as a mole or even a freckle anywhere on her beautifully tanned and hardened body.

We search with little success for a place to dock the *LadyHawk*, finally deciding to drop anchor in the middle of the bay.

The Chart House Restaurant on Glorietta Bay (originally built in 1887) is a Victorian-style, two-story structure with a room-sized cupola—complete with viewing decks on all sides sitting atop its roof—and was originally built as a template for workers to practice on before constructing the actual Hotel Del Coronado across the street, which they built in 1888 in under a year. It later became the first headquarters for the Scripps Institution of Oceanography and converted to the fourth restaurant in the Chart House chain in 1968. The dining room was downstairs, bar upstairs—all overlooking the pristine bay.

I had first visited the restaurant during my stay at the Hotel Del, a fine-dining establishment with a combination of elegance and warmth, a beautiful view of the bay through its glass walls, and lots of highly varnished dark wood. The nostalgic odor of old wood mixed with the salty sea air and nautical décor had immediately pleased all my senses, and I had visited often during my two-week stay at the Del years before.

It is late afternoon as I row the dingy toward the Chart House dock, tie up, and head inside. The restaurant is sparsely populated as we manage to secure two stools at the end of the bar next to the bayside windows, affording us a perfect setting for what is promising to be quite a special evening.

After consuming a couple of drinks, we are thoroughly enjoying each other's company—a bit of gentle touching and admiring looks into each other's eyes, equally feeling out the exact nature of our relationship and where it may be taking us. On the outer edge of my peripheral vision, I observe a dark-haired gentleman emerging from the small circular stairway leading up from downstairs. As his face comes into view, I am somehow not surprised: *It's the KEEPER!*

He glances in my direction, giving no expression of recognition and proceeds to the far end of the bar.

It is what I have signed up for. It will not only never be over for me but rather will always be just beginning, for his presence is signaling a new, and what is sure to be, deadly mission ahead.

Waiting an appropriate amount of time, I excuse myself from Linda and head for the restroom located at the far end of the bar, just past where the KEEPER is sitting with his Stolis rocks. As I am about to pass behind him, he reaches for his wallet and *accidentally* drops it on the floor in front of me. As he attempts to come off his barstool to retrieve it, I say, "I got it, sir." As I'm picking it up, I observe a business card purposely placed in a vertical position within the wallet exposing the "EPER1" at the visible end of the card. I slip the card out and into my shirt pocket, then rise and hand him the wallet.

"Thank you very much, sir," he says as I hand it to him.

"No problem," I reply as I continue to the restroom.

Once securely locked in one of the stalls, I retrieve the card. On the backside are the numbers: 01/12/13/41/25-11/51/9/9/4 -X31/15om.

It's code. I had committed the decoding formula to memory years before, had used it on several occasions, and could translate mentally in seconds.

As I tear up the card into the smallest possible pieces and flush it down the toilet, I am just slightly surprised at the "high profile" of the target, only momentarily questioning how this particular individual could be a sanctioned hit at the highest level and immediately remembering "it is not for me to question, but rather to execute the order."

The "X" indicates a disappearance—"nobody" is ever to be found, and the "om" designates the exact day the mission is to be carried out. In this instance, it is exactly thirty days from today, June 30, 1975.

Knowing instinctively that I cannot show even the slightest change of mood or emotion as I pass behind the KEEPER and return to Linda, I immediately shift my demeanor and mental state back to one of a typical day sailor on a weekend sabbatical with a new and excitingly beautiful woman and touch her gently on the shoulder as I return to my bar stool.

As the dinner hour approaches, we decide to dine at the bar. Our seats are the best in the house. Both the dining room downstairs and the bar have filled up as the dinner hour has arrived.

Knowing where the word *tip* originated—it was an acronym derived from "To Insure Promptness"—I have long been accustomed to *tipping* when the bartender delivers my first drink *to ensure*, in this case, *great service*. I hand him a $100 bill when he delivers our first drinks asking him to run us a tab, put the $100 in his pocket, and keep an eye on us. He not only holds up his part with great service, but he also decides we are his type of people and becomes very friendly with us. I believe the $100 bill got his attention, but Linda's beauty and her friendly personality held it!

The 1:00-a.m. hour finds Frank (our bartender), two of the waitresses, Linda, and me capping off the night doing lines, drinking beer, and smoking dope in the cupola that sits atop the restaurant. It is the beginning of a very memorable weekend.

The Target

The target of this mission is extremely high profile, and the mission is as *deep black* as it gets, except perhaps for my very first mission, which was as riddling as it was dangerous and high profile. Given the terms of my original contract, the kill contradicted who I was led to believe I was working for.

An unsolved conundrum!

The target disappeared on the date specified.

The body has never been found, and the mystery will never be solved.

Ashes to ashes, dust to dust.

As for Linda, we had a wonderful love affair for months. She even moved in for a time. Then one day, it happened as it always has; I awoke in the morning and wanted her out of my life. She had no idea what had happened, and neither did I.

It got ugly, and I removed her from my life while sparing hers.

THE CASTABELLO CONNECTION

"You Tim Hawk?"

The question comes from the far end of the bar. He is a huge black man, well dressed—suit and tie, very businesslike with an underlying sense of evil just beneath the surface. I am instantly on high alert. *Who is he?*

I was at the bar at the Stardust Country Club just blocks removed from my Mission Valley offices.

"Who's asking?"

"Names Ernie. Need a word with you. Mind if I slide down there on that stool next to you?"

"Not my stool. Help yourself."

As he stands up, I make him out to be about six feet eight, 300 plus pounds of potentially dangerous very dark skinned African American, and most definitely a heavyweight—in whatever his field of expertise is. My first guess is that he is mob-connected, as opposed to government, or from my past.

As he overwhelms the stool next to me, he begins.

"I represent the Castabello family out of Palm Springs, and we are looking for and have reason to believe that you may know the whereabouts of a certain woman who goes by the name of Roxzanne Stillwell."

Even in death, she lives on.

The Castabello family is known to me. They are the Italian arm of organized crime in Riverside County, California, headquartered out of Palm Springs, disguised as entrepreneurs owning several hotels and restaurants—The Canyon Hotel, Zelda's, and F. Scott's restaurants, to name a few.

During the time of Roxzanne, we had traveled to Palm Springs for what I had thought was a weekend flyer and turned out to be a drug deal. We stayed at the Canyon Hotel, dined at F. Scott's—a very chic, upscale establishment named after the famous author F. Scott Fitzgerald and themed around his drunken gentlemanly conduct. It boasted a high-end menu, and everything in the restaurant was black and white—symbolic of the black tuxedo and white shirt, which was F. Scott's signature dress and the current price of admission.

We partied into the morning hours at Zelda's, which stood right next door. It was, at the time, the number-one nightclub in the Springs—two stories of glitz, glitter, and neon lights—and it rocked to the beat of bands like Fleetwood Mac and Jim Morrison's The Doors. It was designed and furnished to honor F. Scott's wife, Zelda, a flapper in the 1920s when F. Scott met her. She loved the fast lane of the Jazz Age and lived it, while F. Scott sat nearby and drank himself into a stupor each night, fighting whatever the demons were that haunted him. His genius side wrote now-famous American novels such as *The Great Gatsby* and *The Last Tycoon* when his creative juices were flowing. Unfortunately, this genius would not be recognized until after his death.

We had dined at F. Scott's and stayed till closing time. When the lights were dimmed and the doors were locked, the two Canadian brothers Peter and Ron, who fronted the restaurants for the "family," came over to our table and sat down. They poured out several grams of pure Peruvian flake cocaine on the recently cleaned, glass-topped dining table, chopped, sectioned, and laid out several lines in front of Roxzanne and me as well as themselves. They then handed a rolled-up $100 bill to Roxzanne and another one to me and began the conversation, looking, of course, directly at Roxzanne.

"Two keys will cost you $40,000 as agreed, baby. Yes?"

"Yes," Roxzanne said.

"Good. You have the money with you?" asked Peter.

"Peter—baby!" replied Roxzanne. "How long have we been doing business together, four, maybe five years now?"

"Give or take," said Peter.

"So, at which point in our relationship did you decide I was just another dumb bitch?"

All three of us just smiled respectfully, and I thought once again, *God, you gotta love this chic. As ballsy as she is beautiful! She's never trying to be cool; she simply defines cool.*

"Apologies," said Peter.

"Accepted," said Roxzanne.

"Bring the coke to our hotel room at the Canyon at 2 a.m. The money should arrive by then."

How clever is this chic, insinuating there is no money here or at the hotel? Perfectly paranoid for her business.

"Fine," replied Ron as he looked at his watch, "12:25 a.m. However, I have an offer for you. You can have the two keys for $40,000 as agreed, or you can purchase five keys for $75,000."

Roxzanne stared at Ron, then Peter.

"That is a very attractive offer, but I am not in a position to handle that amount." She then turned to me and said, "How about it, baby? In for a penny, in for a pound?"

I smiled affectionately at her and turned to Peter and Ron, looking from one to the other.

"One hundred thousand for ten keys."

The sideways smile I received from Roxzanne was worth about $500,000.

"No fucking way," said Peter.

"Ten for $120,000," said Ron.

I hesitated the proper amount of time before putting out my hand to Peter. He shook it with a nod, then to Ron, whose firm handshake and appreciative smile sealed the deal.

"I could not help but think *in for a gram, in for a kilo*! And $12,000 a kilo was a steal for Roxzanne, who would cut it and easily quadruple the $120,000 within the next sixty days. Good times!

That had been then. This is now.

"We know you used to partner up with her, also that you guys broke it off a while back. But with a hot piece of ass like Roxzanne, we figured you may just be going back to the old swimming hole for a quick dip now and then, yeah?"

"To tell you the truth, *Ernie*, I truly wish I was "still taking an occasional dip in the old swimming hole," as you so eloquently put it. But I haven't seen that bitch since I motherfucked her so bad one night on the phone that she disappeared from my life. Guess she just couldn't handle the ass chewin'!"

This is comical—*a mob boss chasin' after a ghost*. Why not?

"That's a nice story, but I think you know where she is," he says as he rises from his stool and bids me farewell.

This will not be the last I will see of Big Ernie!

D-DAY

As I speed across a black and empty desert at over 90 mph on a predetermined and cleared path, distancing myself from the coming explosion, visions of death and mayhem cloud my mind.

Suddenly, as if by design, they appear—their mystical glow lighting my way through the bone-chilling winter night of Death Valley. Four mounted and winged warriors, two on my left flank, two on my right flank.

A surrealistic feeling of comfort and safety overwhelm me as I rocket through the night. And there it is, three minutes and a mile and a half into my flight, the sky explodes into an orange and purple and black and yellow firestorm. Memories of Vietnam consume me. It seems almost like I am not present, as if I am floating aimlessly somewhere in the Etherworld, being carried onward by the winged warriors.

Suddenly, I'm back!

Who the fuck are these guys? Are they real? Am I?

Cave Creek, 2020

"Are you?"

"Sir?" asks the reporter.

"Real? Are you real?"

"Of course, sir. I'm Dave Bauer with the *San Diego Union* newspaper, remember? You called me and said you had a story to tell."

"Why are you still here? Have you not heard enough to realize what you are hearing puts me in danger and subsequently puts you in my sights?"

"I do, sir; however, I figured you must be dying or something, and you wanted to reveal yourself before you go."

The old man removes his cell phone from his shirt pocket and sends a text to his bartender downstairs to bring him another Miller Lite.

In the Shadow of the Black is the legal name of his saloon, known to locals simply as "The Black," so named for its location at the foot of Black Mountain, elevation 3,403 ft.

When the old man's beer arrives, the younger man cannot help but notice the attractive woman who is delivering it—dressed in tight-fitting jeans that she most definitely knows how to fill, cowboy boots, and a loose-fitting, very expensive-looking, white silk shirt. He grades her a 9½ on the 10 scale and only because there are no 10s. He estimates her to be somewhere in her mid- to upper 30s. Even given the obvious age disparity, she seems the perfect fit for the old man as she leans over and kisses him while setting his beer on the table next to the .357 revolver and suggestively asks, "You need anything else, baby?"

"I'm good, Ali," he states.

As she is leaving, Ali smiles and touches the old man gently on the shoulder, then shoots a look at the young man that sends a chill clear to his soul and gives him pause to wonder if he will live to write the fascinating story he is being told. At the same time, he wonders why he has been summoned to hear it. This "old man" does not appear to be sick and dying, nor does he seem like he is ready to die any time soon.

"I'm not sure," says the old man, "if it was at the coffin or the cemetery, but I am most assuredly certain that it was one of the two!"

"Sir?" says the reporter.

"The exact moment in time, son. The exact moment in time that my heart went to war with my soul and the ability to truly love and care were gone forever.

"In fact, I was so steeped in self-pity and bitterness that it took me twenty-plus years to come to the realization that 'I,' not God, had killed my child. Sitting here now, reunited with the God I knew as a child and having been responsible for literally hundreds of deaths in a variety of ways from a bullet to the back of the head to detonating explosions that killed hundreds in an instant—men, women, children, dogs, cats, you name it—I killed it. I regret only one kill: the execution I performed by doing nothing."

Pop! A single shot shocks the quiet.

THE END
of
THE BEGINNING

* * * * * * * *

THE DEATH VALLEY TIMES

December 26, 1982

"Furnace Creek Inn Explosion Kills over 450—No Survivors"

* * * * * * * *

RIVERSIDE PRESS

December 27, 1982

"Furnace Creek Inn Tragedy, Cause under Investigation"

* * * * * * * *

SAN BERNARDINO TRIBUNE

December 29, 1982

"Mexican Mafia Being Investigated in Connection with Death Valley Explosion"

* * * * * * * *

LOS ANGELES TIMES

December 30, 1982

Death Valley Tragedy Update: "Cartels Run for Cover"

* * * * * * * *

SAN DIEGO UNION-TRIBUNE

December 31, 1982

"Local Entrepreneur's Remains Found at Furnace Creek Inn"

The remains of Tim Hawk, San Diego entrepreneur and owner of California's largest independent auto leasing brokerage, were among the 482 souls retrieved from what appears to have been a cartel revenge hit that completely demolished the Furnace Creek Inn in Death Valley on Christmas Day. Apparently, Mr. Hawk was on holiday at the inn.

EPISODE II

Coming soon . . .

The Soul of a Man
The Rebirth

SAN DIEGO UNION-TRIBUNE

January 20, 1983

"Rick Hawk, Brother of Tim Hawk, assumes Control of California's Largest Auto Leasing Brokerage"

Still shaken by the loss of his brother in the horrific Furnace Creek Inn tragedy and a deadly fire at his home on the Isle of Man off the coast of Ireland—where his hands and face were badly burned when he unsuccessfully attempted to rescue his seven-month-old son—Rick Hawk has taken the reins of the company that was on the verge of monopolizing the automobile leasing industry in the state of California before his brother's death.

Made in the USA
Monee, IL
20 January 2022